"You really are the Marquis of Grantsby?"

Doubt showed in Juliana's face as she asked the question.

He sighed. "I should have told you before Juliana, but I feared it would blight our relationship. Yes, I am Miles Harcourt, Marquis of Grantsby."

Her heart began to pound. Slowly the pieces began to fit together. He had tricked her!

"And now suppose you tell me who *you* really are?" Miles ignored her sudden intake of breath. "Don't look so put-upon. I want the truth."

"But I've told you. My name is Juliana Penridge. I am recently widowed—"

"Oh, come now, Juliana. Don't take me for a fool. I know nobility when I meet it. And wouldn't it be less embarrassing to confess now, before I take you to Grantsby Hall and introduce you to my mother?"

Books by Phyllis Taylor Pianka

HARLEQUIN REGENCY ROMANCE
5–MIDNIGHT FOLLY

HARLEQUIN INTRIGUE
16–MIDSUMMER MADNESS

Don't miss any of our special offers. Write to us at the
following address for information on our newest releases.

Harlequin Reader Service
901 Fuhrmann Blvd., P.O. Box 1397, Buffalo, NY 14240
Canadian address: P.O. Box 603,
Fort Erie, Ont. L2A 5X3

DAME FORTUNE'S FANCY

PHYLLIS TAYLOR PIANKA

Harlequin Books

TORONTO • NEW YORK • LONDON
AMSTERDAM • PARIS • SYDNEY • HAMBURG
STOCKHOLM • ATHENS • TOKYO • MILAN

To Edwin Pianka,
with a hug to Dame Fortune
for sending him to me.
And to Lenore and Gene Salefski,
with gratitude and affection.

Published March 1987
ISBN 0-373-31017-X

CHAPTER ONE

JULIANA PENRIDGE STUDIED a spoon-shaped arrangement of stars through the leaded window of the silent country house as she idly smoothed the lavender and bayberry scented quilt over her hips. What an odd turn her life had taken in this winter of 1815. Except for a random twist of fate, she would at this minute be aboard the *Empress Elaine*, bound for the West Indies. Instead, she was her own mistress, at the beck and call of no mortal man. And she was happy.

The stranger in the bedroom across the hall groaned as he tried to turn over in his narrow bed, and Juliana leaped up to rush to his side. She touched his brow, but it was only slightly warm, and she began to chuckle.

"My own mistress, indeed," she said aloud. "I'm sore afraid I still have you to contend with, my rugged friend." Yet even as she said the words, Juliana knew that she didn't mind one single whit.

She checked the pad of lint on his head and sighed with satisfaction that it showed no new trace of blood. Cleansing the wound had opened it for a time, but it now appeared to have closed. She pulled the quilt around him and tucked it close to his chin, as if he were a child and she his mother. Indeed, although he must have been in his thirties, in his present state of vulnerability there was much of the child about him. Dark brows and heavily fringed lashes softened the strong jawline, which was shadowed now with a few days' growth of beard.

A whimsical smile tugged at the corners of her mouth as she gazed down at the moustache that graced his upper lip. Juliana had sometimes wondered what it would feel like to kiss a moustached man. Did she dare? Surely he would never know.

She bent slowly, her hair swinging like a golden cloud from the brushing she had given it. His breath fluttered against her face as she leaned closer, but he did not stir. Ever so softly she touched his mouth in a gentle caress. His hair smelled of the sea, and his moustache rasped against her skin. She caught her breath and straightened abruptly, aghast and a little ashamed of her own temerity.

Indeed! It was unseemly behaviour to take advantage of the poor man. She shouldn't have been so forward. But at the same time a small part of her tingled from the excitement of her daring.

Common sense had always ruled Juliana's life— that, along with modesty, diligence to one's duty and, of course, honesty. It had often irked Juliana that the standards for deportment were so much more rigid for her than they were for her brother, Jules. Of course, he was a male and four years her senior. According to their father, men must learn early in life to take command. Jules had learned the hard way and now lay at the bottom of the sea, a victim of the war with the French.

Juliana blinked quickly, bringing her gaze back to the man on the bed. She studied the sharply chiseled line of his jaw, knowing instinctively that he had also been taught the lesson of male dominance.

She resented the role she had been forced to play and wondered how different it might have been if her mother had lived. As it was, her father, the fifth son of a German count, had given her over at the age of ten to the strict discipline of a headmistress. Between the death of Juliana's mother and the time of her marriage at eighteen, she, Juliana, had attended Miss Margaret Haverstock's School for Young Ladies. Her father had not lived to see the consummation of her marriage to Cedric. It was just as well. Even he would have been appalled at the treatment she had received at her husband's hands, not to mention the short time it took Cedric to go through what little money her father had left her.

Despite her weariness, Juliana knew that sleep would be a long time coming, and she had left the drapes open to enable her to see the sky. Experience gained from long nights waiting for Cedric to return from his gaming tables had taught her how to pass the lonely hours. Now the waiting was over. Cedric had pushed fate too far, and she was widowed at the age of twenty-two.

Another day had passed before Juliana was absolutely certain her patient was on the mend. His fever had subsided, but he still slept almost continuously, waking only long enough to sip some broth. His name was Miles, Miles Harcourt. Beyond that he remained a subject for conjecture, and Juliana was forced to bide her time until the man was ready to talk.

After awhile she went to bed, satisfied that she had done all she could to make him comfortable. His newly laundered clothing lay dried and neatly folded on the chair by his bed, and Juliana was weary to the point of exhaustion. Four times she had gone to the cistern to draw water to drink and for their ablutions. When she had felt confident to leave his side for a few minutes, she had scrubbed and scoured the kitchen and scullery as token payment for her sin of trespass. Besides, it had helped to stay busy. There had been less time to consider her tenuous future.

The stranger—Miles, she corrected her thoughts—still slept soundly when she got up to check on him. Perhaps tomorrow would bring definite signs of recovery. Miles Harcourt. The name suited his appearance: handsome in a rugged sort of way but not overly pretentious.

She sat in a chair for a few moments to watch him sleep, and before she knew it, she had drifted off.

It was the creak of a floorboard that wakened her. She opened her eyes cautiously, her heart pounding with such vigor she was certain it must be heard. It took a moment for her eyes and her senses to adjust themselves. When they did, she became aware of a denser shadow blocking out the light from the moon. It was Miles. He was standing there beside her chair, looking down at her.

It was pure reflex to want to scream, but she managed to hold back. Best to feign sleep and see what he was about. For an agonizing moment he stood looking down at her. Then he slowly reached down and grasped a strand of her hair, which lay fanned out against her shoulder. With the gentlest of movement he curled it around his finger and stroked it with his thumb, as if testing a length of treasured silk. The gesture was profoundly unsettling. When Juliana could stand it no more, she spoke.

"Mr. Harcourt, I think you should return to your bed. You are far too weakened to be wandering around. You can't afford to get a chill."

He sucked in his breath, and the sound was loud in the stillness of the night. A moment later he had pulled the coverlet over himself and sat down on the edge of the cot. The strength of his voice belied his weakness.

"Just who the devil are you?" he asked. "And how, in the name of everything I hold sacred, did I get here?"

She stood, carefully pulling her dressing gown around her. "My name is Juliana Penridge. And as to how you got here, I discovered you unconscious along the grass verge in the lane leading to this house. In addition to exposure to the storm, you appeared to be suffering from a nasty blow on the head."

His hand went to the bandage, and he winced. "Yes, I remember now. I was set upon by highwaymen. One of them struck me. How long have I been here? Did they take my horse and seabag?"

She nodded. "I would assume so. I saw nothing when I found you Thursday morning, two days ago." She felt along the floor for her slippers. "Are you in pain? Is your vision blurred?"

"I think not, though it's difficult to tell in the dark. It is dark, isn't it? I haven't suddenly gone near blind?"

She could hear the humor in his voice, and she smiled. "Rest assured, the light you see is from the moon. The blow to your head must have been severe. Has it affected your memory?" She was hoping that he would say something that would give her a clue to his background, but when he spoke, she was disappointed.

"The last thing I remember before the ruffians attacked me was reading about the newly imposed stamp duties that raised the cost of the newspapers by fourpence."

"Um. The law passed last spring, but the newspapers are still full of it. The radicals seem to think it's a Tory plot to keep 'hostile propaganda' out of the hands of the common people who can't afford to spend sevenpence for a newspaper."

He lay back against the pillow. "You watch. It's going to result in a blackmarket press."

"It already has," she assured him. "Cabbett's *Political Register* and Thomas Wooler's *Black Dwarf* are causing quite a strain in political circles."

"Too bad James Gillray isn't alive. He would have had a fine time drawing his political cartoons."

Juliana smiled as she remembered the monsterlike caricatures that had made Gillray famous. And she was also pleased to have reasonable proof that Mr. Harcourt was in full command of his memory. By the time she had found the packet of gypsy matches on the nightstand, lit the lamp and adjusted the wick, her hands had steadied, but as she turned to face his close scrutiny, they again began to tremble. Apparently he didn't notice because when he spoke his voice sounded confused.

"Judging from the looks of the room, we are in the servants' quarters, but you don't sound like a servant. And that dressing gown must have cost a small ransom." He ran his hand across his chin. "You've told me your name, and now would you be so kind as to tell me just who you are and what you are doing here?"

Juliana was a bit put off by his aggressive manner, but she attributed it to his condition. "Surely it could wait until morning. You are not as strong as . . ."

He shook his head impatiently. "Nonsense. I am perfectly fit, and I insist you provide me with some answers." He sighed. "Forgive me. I didn't mean to sound so gruff. Be assured, you have nothing to fear from me, but I wonder, are you then a servant of the household?"

She walked over to the window and rested her hand against the cool windowpane. "No. I am not a servant. I chanced upon the house in much the same manner as you. Three days ago I was traveling by stage coach to London when the coach in which I was riding broke an axle when it struck a pothole during the storm. The passengers were eventually transferred to another coach to continue the journey, but alas, before we were five miles on our way, the coachman informed us that we must each pay an additional sum of money. Unfortunately I did not have sufficient funds to waste, so I was left with my baggage to stand in the lane in the middle of the rainstorm.''

She spread her hands. ''I was destitute. There was nothing in sight save this deserted country estate, so I took refuge here in the servants' wing of the house.''

He nodded as he began to understand. ''And that was when?''

''Three days ago. It was the following morning when I started off to continue my journey to London that I discovered you in an unconscious state at the side of the road. I managed to rouse you enough to help you walk to the house, and...well, here we are.''

His voice took on an edge. ''Then it was you who divested me of my boots and breeches?''

She felt her face redden, but she lifted her chin. ''Mr. Harcourt! I could hardly allow you to go to bed in such a filthy condition, if not for your own sake, then for the sake of our host, whoever he might be.''

He looked around the clean but austerely furnished room. ''Since you took it upon yourself to claim sanctuary, how is it that you chose to use the servants' quarters when the master's apartments would have been much more comfortable?''

''Indeed! How can you ask such a thing? Isn't it enough that I come uninvited and partake of food and shelter without so much as a by your leave? I intend to make restitution when I find a position and save some money, but I certainly do not want to become any further indebted than is necessary.''

''Doubtless the nob can afford it.'' His hand dropped to the coverlet, and her gaze was drawn to the fine dark hair that curled around his wrist. Judging from his clothing and his remark about a seabag, she had assumed he was a sailor, but his voice and bearing gave her cause to wonder. He studied her face as if to watch her reaction to his words.

"Who would be the wiser if you were to help yourself to whatever is here? You said yourself the house is deserted."

Juliana was appalled. "If you continue to talk like that, I will regret having rescued you from the storm. Suffice it to say that I could not in good conscience disturb anything that is not necessary to our survival." She tucked her hands into the full arms of her dressing gown and walked back toward the lamp. "I daresay we can manage well enough in the servants' quarters until we are ready to leave. Since our being here is of my doing, I must insist that you make every effort to follow my wishes in this respect."

He bent his arm and tucked a hand beneath his head. "That is an order?"

Juliana knew a baited question when she heard one. She strongly suspected that this man was accustomed to giving orders instead of taking them. Her voice softened.

"Consider it a request, if you prefer. Needless to say, we should not need to tarry here for more than a day or two. Given enough rest and adequate food, you should be able to travel soon."

She studied his face, trying to get beyond the challenge of his eyes, which were deep cobalt blue. "Were you on your way to London when you were accosted?"

He sighed and stroked his beard. "In a manner of speaking. I've just returned from the New World, and I have things to attend to before I make London. And you? Isn't it odd for a woman of your breeding to be traveling alone?"

"It is perfectly proper, I assure you. I am recently widowed and was to have taken a position as companion to Lady Penelope Cromwell on her journey to the West Indies. Unfortunately, it is probably too late now. The *Empress Elaine* will no doubt have departed long before I can reach London."

"Then what will you do?"

"I don't know, but I will find some means of support." She reached for a mobcap and put it on her head, taking care to tuck the corn-silk colored curls inside. "And you, Mr. Harcourt. You say you are bound eventually for London? What was it that brought you to this deserted region?"

He started to speak and then apparently thought better of it. After an interminable pause, he shrugged. "Yes, I will soon go to London, for as they say, 'Our fortunes may take us hither and yon, but a Londoner's heart always goes home.'" He smiled then turned onto his side.

"But the hour is late, Mrs. Penridge, and I fear I am more trouble than is necessary. Would it not be wise if we were to sleep again before dawn?"

Juliana was flustered. "Yes, I don't know what I was thinking of to let us go on like this. Your strength depends upon sleep and nourishment. Would you enjoy a cup of broth before you go to sleep?"

"I think not, though I am in your debt. I have the feeling you have kept me well-fed, even though I was unaware at the time."

She smiled. "I did manage to force some food down your throat, though you complained most harshly about the barley soup."

He laughed. "That comes as no surprise. I detest barley."

"A pity. Since it is the one thing we seem to have in abundance."

"You found scant food in the cellar?" He sounded surprised.

"Oh, there is an ample supply of preserved foods: currants, smoked hams, and a wide variety of things. I simply tried to avoid using anything that might be considered a luxury. Doubtless the owner and his staff are in London for the season and will return in due time. I wouldn't want them to be caught short when they would naturally expect a full larder."

"Considerate, but not appropriate under the circumstances. Most people take what they can when there is little chance of being caught."

Her voice turned cold. "Be that as it may, I do not intend to take advantage. Since there is nothing you need, I will turn out the light and bid you good-night."

"Good night, Mrs. Penridge."

As she turned down the wick to extinguish the lamp, she heard him settle down beneath the covers. A moment later she returned to her room and began to remove her dressing gown but had second thoughts and simply lay down without taking it off. True, he was still weak and seemed to pose no threat to her. Still, it was better to be safe than sorry.

Either her patient was still very tired, or he was being most considerate of her. He fell asleep almost immediately and roused her only once during the night when he cried out in his sleep. She rushed to his side, fearing the worst, but he did not waken, and Juliana decided it was nothing more than an unpleasant dream.

When Juliana rose later that same morning, storm clouds, seen through the kitchen window, continued to do battle with the distant hills. Ancient beech trees dropped their branches close to the ground from the weight of the water that had saturated the land for the past four days.

How she loved this place! True, the grounds suffered from neglect. The ancient stonework was yellowed now and pitted by contest with storms and grasping tendrils of ivy vines. Yet somehow, that same evidence of aging lent a mellowness that spoke to Juliana of contentment.

Yonder, toward the east, lay an orchard that, come spring, would be carpeted with bluebells and red campion. This was sheep country, dotted with meadows and hedgerows, thickets, little valleys and steep-sided combes. She wanted to embrace it. To populate it with long-necked geese and cackling hens... and children to run in the meadows and drink from the lion's-head fountain she had discovered set in the stone wall near the tangled herb garden.

But she had to be practical. No time now for fanciful daydreams. She had to think of her future.

How fortunate she had been to find shelter during this time. It would have been impossible to hire transport to London out here in the middle of the country, even if she had the funds to do so. And now there were the two of them. He had said he was going to London. She put the tea safe down with a clatter.

Indeed! Until this moment it had not occurred to her, but Mr. Harcourt had neatly sidestepped the question when she had asked him about what he planned to do once he regained his strength. Had he been deliberately evasive? Surely not. Not unless he had something to hide. In truth, he might himself be one of the highwaymen he talked about. The thought did little to curb her increasing anxiety.

Once the fire began to burn brightly in the grate, she put the kettle on to boil. While she was waiting, she took the pins from her hair and let it fall in a dusky gold cascade around her shoulders. Finding her hairbrush in the bottom of her reticule, she bent down and began to brush her hair forward over her head until it crackled with hidden fire.

Hearing a movement behind her, she caught her breath, then turned quickly to see Miles Harcourt leaning against the open door. His face and voice reflected his amusement.

"I can see I spoke in haste last night when I first awoke."

Juliana quickly gathered her hair into a wad and stuffed it beneath her mobcap. "I . . . I'm sure I don't know to what you refer, Mr. Harcourt."

"My wits were not as sharp as they might have been, but I recall saying that you had nothing to fear from me. Seeing you with your hair spread out around you, like clouds turned gold by the sunrise, makes me realize that despite my weakness I am still a man.''

"Indeed, I had no doubt about that from the start.'' As soon as the words were out of her mouth, Juliana regretted them. He was well aware that she had stripped him down to his smallclothes. He raised his eyebrows, but before he had a chance to speak, she quickly turned away. "I simply mean that your beard is quite heavy.''

He chuckled. "Ah, yes, the beard. I shall have to find a razor and scrape it off. I had intended to shave once I arrived at my destination.''

"Which is?''

"London. Didn't I say that earlier?''

She shrugged. "Yes, but London is a large city.''

"Indeed, as large as my interests. I have many places to go in London and much to do.''

Juliana felt a prickle of irritation, and she turned around to face the window lest it show. He was being deliberately obtuse. Well, be that as it may, it was none of her concern. Given a change in the weather, she would be well on her way by this time tomorrow.

But the thought left her sad. Cedric had been right. She was an odd one. Here she was in the middle of nowhere with a man who might be a highwayman, and she was loath to leave. Unlike Cedric, she placed little belief in fate, but it would help if she had some idea what Dame Fortune had in store for her this time.

He broke into her reverie. "Once again, Mrs. Penridge, I see I am in your debt. I found my clothing laundered and neatly folded next to my bed.'' He looked down at the coarse fustians. "You are most kind."

"It was nothing, Mr. Harcourt. I'm sure you would have done the same for me under those circumstances."

His eyes twinkled dangerously. "Indeed, Mrs. Penridge, it would have been my pleasure to do as much for you. Consider me at your service any time."

She gripped the back of a chair. "Mr. Harcourt, you are deliberately twisting my words, and I'll thank you to keep your innuendos to yourself."

He chuckled and moved closer. Before she knew what he intended, he pulled the mobcap from her hair and let the curls tumble down over her shoulders. His fingers grazed her arm as he picked up a curl and shaped it between his fingers.

"Don't put the cap back on. Your hair is like heavy silk. From what I have guessed, there are just the two of us here. Surely there is no need for such strict propriety."

Despite her attempt to keep it steady, her voice wavered. "Your logic is twisted, Mr. Harcourt. It is because there are just the two of us that there is an even greater need for propriety."

His face clouded, and his voice took on a note of concern. "Forgive me. You said you are recently widowed. Are you then in deep mourning for your former husband?"

She felt her face flush. How in God's name was she to answer such a question? True, she had donned the traditional black crepe, but in all honesty, Cedric had meant little to her. If truth be told, she had feared and sometimes hated him.

"You hesitate, Mrs. Pendridge. Do I detect something less than grief in your feelings?"

She lifted her chin in defiance. "Suffice it to say that I am in mourning for my husband. I trust that you are gentleman enough to respect that."

He moved close to her until she could see the glinting lights in his cobalt blue eyes. "I respect any true grief, Mrs. Penridge." He picked up her mobcap from the table where he had dropped it, folding it carefully with his hands. The gesture was so gentle and so unexpected that for a moment Juliana was thoroughly unsettled.

CHAPTER TWO

JULIANA WAS TAKEN ABACK by her own tremulous feelings. Only once before had she ever been tempted to reach out to touch a man. It was when she was fourteen and she had been infatuated with Mr. Worthington, the music teacher at Miss Haverstock's School for Young Ladies. She had been wise enough not to make a fool of herself then, and she wasn't about to do so now with a perfect stranger.

Perfect...how appropriate the words were. Mr. Harcourt was indeed a fine specimen of a man, now that he was dressed in clean clothing.

He caught her studying his face and was apparently amused. He chuckled knowingly, and Juliana stiffened as she reached for her mobcap and placed it firmly on her head.

"Mr. Harcourt, do behave like a gentleman. Will you have tea while I'm preparing a bowl of porridge?"

"Porridge." He wrinkled his nose. "I haven't eaten that since I was a child. Have we no bread?"

"You forget that we are in a deserted house. Be grateful for what we have, Mr. Harcourt, and the fact that we are alive and well. I shudder to think what might have happened to us had we not been under heaven's care."

He grinned. "You sound like my mother."

"I'll take that as a compliment, however you meant it. Now, as to the tea?"

He made a mock bow. "Tea it is, and while you set it to brew, I'll see what I can find in the larder to deaden the taste of the porridge."

Juliana had set two places at the servants' table in the large oak-beamed kitchen. The room was immaculate with copper pots hanging in neat rows from a beam over an enormous worktable. Food safes, empty now except for bunches of dried herbs and rushes placed inside to keep them smelling sweet, stood on the opposite side. Like most kitchens, it was below stairs, but a partial view of the outside was afforded by narrow rectangular windows near the ceiling. Juliana could see enough to realize it was still raining.

Several doors opened off the room. One led to a hallway that gave access to the living quarters upstairs. There was also the door leading to the cellar storage rooms where, along with boxes and boxes of household supplies, were rows of shelves filled with preserved food. It was only out of desperation for something to eat that Juliana had discovered the room.

Apparently Mr. Harcourt had less trouble searching it out because it seemed he returned in no time, bearing an armload of assorted food. Juliana was appalled.

"Really, Mr. Harcourt, I must protest. We simply cannot do this."

"And why not? I guarantee I shall pay for everything."

"Of course. And just how do you intend to do that? The thieves stole your money and everything of value when you were attacked in the storm."

"Then I shall leave my marker...as you did." He grinned.

"You...you discovered my note?"

"Yes, and charming it was." He pulled it from his pocket and began to read.

Dear Lord of the manor:
I must beg mercy of you, kind sir, in that I have taken it upon myself to intrude into the privacy of your dwelling. Having been forced from my coach by an unscrupulous driver, I found myself in dire straits without protection from the storm. Finding a shutter ajar, I...

"Give me that note!" she demanded as she attempted to snatch it from his hand. She felt her face go hot. "Really, Mr. Harcourt, you are insufferable. Give that to me. I want to put it back under the Chinese vase where they will be sure to find it."

"Never fear. I'll put it back. Look. I've found apricot and raspberry preserves. A goodly dollop might make even porridge seem a treat to the palate." He found a knife and pried the jar open as Juliana sighed with exasperation.

"There's no reasoning with you, since you are so determined to have your own way. Sit down and I shall pour the tea."

He walked over to where she was standing, held her chair and seated her. Juliana was amazed by his courtly manners, but she saw his behavior as just another way of winning her over.

"Thank you, but if you think you can use charm to get your way, I assure you it won't succeed. Either you behave yourself here and restrict your movement to the servants' quarters, or I shall be forced to report you to the local constable."

He threw his head back and laughed. "Juliana Penridge, how innocent you are in the ways of the world. Have you forgotten that you, too, are trespassing? Granted, you are most considerate of your absent host, but in the eyes of the law you are as guilty as you say I am. Tell me, are you ready to spend the rest of your life incarcerated with me in Newgate Prison? Perhaps we could share cells."

She paled. "But I have every intention of paying back whatever I have used. I can't believe that you would..."

"Believe what you like, but don't get in my way. Given enough cause, I may just decide to take you to prison with me. Since we are in this fix together, we might as well enjoy it."

Juliana smoothed the skirt of her black crepe dress, then sighed in frustration. "You are most ungrateful, Mr. Harcourt, but since we shall be taking our leave on the morrow, I rather imagine I shall have to put up with your ways."

He grinned. "Well put, Mrs. Penridge," he said as he seated himself opposite her, then laid a small packet on the table. "Would you enjoy cinnamon in your tea?"

She drew in her breath sharply. "Mr. Harcourt!"

"Come now. This small luxury will not bankrupt our host. Take my word for it."

"Thank you, I prefer to forgo the pleasure."

"Woman, don't be so god-awful namby-pamby. Look at you. You wear that ridiculous cap on top of your head when you should give me the pleasure of seeing your hair. You wear that gloomy black gown when it is plain to see that blue is your color."

Juliana was hurt. Did she truly look so frumpy? She hastened to defend herself. "I have told you I'm in mourning. It would be unseemly for me to wear colors at least for the next ten months."

"Don't you consider that a bit hypocritical? You said in so many words that you didn't love your husband. What happened to him?" A malicious grin lighted his eyes. "I'd be willing to bet he didn't die in bed. What did you do, put arsenic in his porridge?"

Juliana was fuming. "You take too much upon yourself, Mr. Harcourt. It wasn't that I didn't care for Cedric. He had good qualities. He bought many lovely gowns for me and saw that I wanted for nothing while he was alive."

"Indeed? If that were true, then why is it you find yourself alone and destitute? You yourself said that you needed to find a position."

Juliana shifted uncomfortably on the wooden chair. She didn't want to talk about her problems, and least of all about Cedric, but there was a softening in his gaze that probed beyond his mocking tone of voice. She sighed.

"Cedric had a penchant for the gambling tables. He entered into a wager with the Earl of Fordyce and..."

"Don't tell me—I can guess. He lost everything."

Juliana's eyes blazed. "Indeed not. If truth be told, he won the wager, but before he could carry his winnings home, he was set upon by thieves and beaten to death. The earl somehow managed to retrieve the papers he had signed over to my husband and persuade the witnesses to testify on his behalf. The earl is a scoundrel, everyone knows that, but I was unable to find a single man to witness on my late husband's behalf. Our home and everything in it was taken over by the earl and his henchmen."

"And all you have left is what you are wearing?"

"Very nearly. When I was forced from the coach, they also threw my trunks to the ground, but I lacked the strength to fetch them here. I left them concealed in a dense thicket at the end of the lane."

"The rain will ruin them if we leave them there. Later on I will take the cart and fetch them here."

"I can't let you do that. You are still not recovered."

"Don't be ridiculous. I have the strength of ten men. Do I look as if I'm about to faint dead away?"

Juliana's face grew warm. "You look reasonably fit."

"'Reasonably'? Indeed, Mrs. Penridge, you are stingy with your compliments."

She replied with a tartness that surprised even her. "No doubt you've had more than your share of attention from the ladies. I see no need for me to fawn over you.''

"Now there's a backhanded compliment, but I suppose it will have to do for the present. Drink your tea, Mrs. Penridge, before it cools.''

She sipped slowly, then sighed with pure pleasure. The pilfered cinnamon added both a fragrance and a spice that soothed and delighted. He smiled at her obvious enjoyment, and his voice was low and teasing.

"Breaking the rules can be pleasurable now and then. Am I not right, Mrs. Penridge?''

She gave him a look intended to wither, but at the last minute her mouth turned up at the corners, and she smiled despite herself.

TRUE TO HIS WORD, Miles Harcourt hauled the two heavy trunks out of the rainstorm while she cleaned their dishes and set the kitchen to rights. He brought them into the kitchen just as she was hanging up the porridge pot.

"You hid them well, Mrs. Penridge. I nearly missed them."

"Oh, dear. They look dreadful. What did you do, roll them in the mud?''

"Such gratitude! Have you no idea how heavy they are? I had to roll them to get them onto the cart.''

"Pity. With the strength of ten I thought you would have no trouble at all lifting them in one hand. Had I known your weakened condition, I would have gone after them myself."

He looked surprised. "I'd be careful if I were you, Mrs. Penridge. I don't take well to the needle."

"I can see that," she said, turning his words back on him. "Your appearance leaves much to be desired, despite the fact that I scrubbed your clothing till my skin puckered."

He looked at his worn fustian breeches. "For once I shall have to agree. Why don't we take a tour of the gentleman's quarters and see what the armoires have to offer? Unless I'm wrong, we're bound to find a wardrobe kept here for country wear. Your clothing in the trunks will need to be dried before you can wear them, so you might as well join me in a foray through the house."

"Never. I'd go unclothed before I'd willingly trespass on the family's privacy."

"Now there's a good idea! Under those circumstances I would be only too delighted to bow to your commands."

"You have a vile sense of humor, Mr. Harcourt. What mortal sin am I being punished for that I should deserve you?"

He studied her face for so long that she found it oddly disturbing. His voice was gentle and warm. "Juliana Penridge. Looking into those lovely brown eyes and seeing that exquisitely pink complexion, I know beyond a shadow of a doubt that you are completely without sin."

She was flustered to the point that all she could do was drop her gaze and murmur a thank-you. There was a slight pause, as if time held its breath, and then he spoke triumphantly.

"You see? That just proves a point. My presence here is not at all to be considered punishment. On the contrary, I am your reward for having lived an impeccable life."

He had moved in close as he spoke. Juliana lifted her head and glared straight into his eyes. "Mr. Harcourt, you are without a doubt the most irritating, insufferable, self-centered man I have ever met."

"And you, Mrs. Penridge, have a tongue like a rapier and a temper to match. If you weren't so ugly, I might even fall in love with you."

Her eyes opened wide, and she started to return the insult, but instead she moved quickly away and ran up the back stairs to the safety of the bedroom. A pox on him, she thought to herself. He's made me cry. I thought no man could ever do that to me again. She wiped her eyes on the sleeve of her mourning costume, determined to put an end to the flow of tears. Ugly indeed. She might have nothing else in the world, but she had no reason to apologize for her face and figure. Her appearance and her small inheritance were the main reasons Cedric had married her.

When she glanced at the clouded mirror over the plain wooden chest, Juliana stopped suddenly. Truly, her face was pale, and there were faint purple smudges beneath her eyes. She was a good bit thinner now than she had been before Cedric's death, and the hollows below her cheekbones made faint shadows in the gloom of the day. No one would have guessed that her brother, Jules, used to taunt her about the roses in her cheeks.

Quickly Juliana pinched her cheeks and chewed her lower lips to bring back the color. It helped momentarily. And if she wore the ivory shawl she had packed in the trunk, it would soften the effect of the ugly black dress.

Before she realized what she was doing, Juliana was halfway down the stairway to the kitchen. "Oh, bother!" she whispered. *Why should I try to impress him? He means nothing to me—that is, except for the comfort of another human being during the storm. Human being?* She grimaced at the thought. *I'm not sure the man is even that.* But since she had come this far, she decided she might as well continue on to the kitchen and see how much damage had been done to the contents of her trunks.

As she quietly entered the door to the kitchen, she heard a scraping noise and stopped where she was. The hair stood up on the nape of her neck, but as she cautiously edged closer, she realized that the sound she had heard was Mr. Harcourt attempting to force the lock on one of her trunks. She had been right in the beginning. He was a thief. And now he was trying to steal from her, even after she had saved his life.

Stepping quietly, she reached for a large mallet and stole up behind him, with the mallet poised to strike.

"I wouldn't do that if I were you, Mrs. Penridge," he said without pausing at his work on the lock. "My head hurts enough as it is."

"Then get away from my trunks." Somehow her voice lacked the conviction it should have had, but he stood and looked at her.

"I was only trying to help. I had it in mind to lay your things out to dry. Doubtless they will be damp and musty."

"The trunks are sturdy. I see no reason why anything should be damaged, that is to say unless you've already got your hands on the contents," she added with a touch of malice. "At any rate, I have a key. There is no need to break the lock."

"I wasn't about to break it. I'm an expert at locks and can open most of them without a key."

"I've no doubt that you can. Most thieves have such abilities, so I'm told."

He laughed. "Have it your own way."

As she took the chain from her neck and tried to insert the key, she soon found that the lock was caked with mud and refused to yield. Once again tears of frustration threatened to spill over, but he reached down, took the key from her hand and dipped it into the kettle of hot water. Then he inserted it into the lock, and the key immediately turned.

He had the good grace to allow her the right to open it in privacy. And he was right. Water had penetrated the brassbound wood until everything was damp and musty smelling. If something wasn't done soon, all she owned in the world would be gone.

One by one she lifted the fine garments from their wrappings and laid them on the worktable. There was a fortune in exquisite laces, brocades, velvets, and filmy muslins. Cedric had taken pleasure in dressing his wife in costly gowns and jewels. Most of the jewelry was sold to pay the debtors, but the gowns would have brought little in the way of money. Then, too, she would have needed a fine wardrobe to act as companion to Lady Penelope on their tour of the West Indies. Well, that was in the past, but with the help of heaven she would find another position in a quality household. Appearances meant a great deal. She would need to look her best.

Juliana was at a loss what to do. If she were to leave for London tomorrow, she simply had to get her things dry enough to repack. It was her intention to leave the trunks at the house with a message that she would send a drayman to pick them up as soon as she had a definite address. Even so, she couldn't leave them unpacked.

"Oh, bother! Will this infernal rain never cease?"

"All in good time, Mrs. Penridge."

She turned at the sound of his voice and smiled helplessly. "You were right, I'm afraid. My things are sodden. I am at a loss to know what to do about them. If the sun would only shine, I could place them outside on the bushes to dry."

"Why not hang them in here from the hooks on the beams? We can build a roaring fire in the fireplace, and they will dry in no time."

"By tomorrow, do you think?"

"Why tomorrow?"

She looked surprised. "But tomorrow is when we must leave."

"Why? Does it distress you to share the house with me? Are you frightened?"

"Most certainly not."

He smiled. "Then I take it you have begun to enjoy my company? Even though you find me irritating, insufferable and a heartless prig?"

"I didn't call you a heartless prig," she said.

"Um. So you didn't. Nice to know I'm not a complete failure. Are you saying you might learn to enjoy my company?"

"I already do... when you are sleeping."

"So that's the way it is, eh? Tonight we might be well advised to share the same room, so that you may enjoy my company even more."

"I wouldn't place a wager on it if I were you, Mr. Harcourt."

He laughed. "Congratulations. For once you managed to avoid blushing. Egad. I spoke too soon, or was the reaction merely delayed?"

She turned away. "Why don't you lie down and rest while I take care of my clothing? You don't look well."

"It's the beard. I haven't shaved as yet. Let me help you hang the gowns to dry. Between the two of us we'll make short work of it."

It was useless to argue. As she unpacked and handed the gowns to him, he hung them from the beams, then built a crackling fire in the fireplace to speed the drying.

"Thank you, Mr. Harcourt. They surely will dry tonight."

He pushed out his lower lip. "I doubt it, but does it matter? I have no intention of leaving tomorrow. I can't see the sense in trying to get to London in this uncertain weather. It only makes good sense to wait another day or two."

Juliana protested, but in her heart she knew that staying another day was exactly what she wanted to do. Finally she agreed aloud to think about his suggestion, but the peculiar little twitch of his moustache told her that he already knew what her answer would be.

There was a tense moment for Juliana when he picked up some of her unmentionables. He stood there holding the diaphanous silks in his fingers, and his eyes crinkled with amusement.

"Such delicate lace to protect such treasures. 'Tis indeed remarkable that..."

She didn't allow him to finish but snatched them from him and gave him a withering look. "I think I can manage, thank you. There is no need for you to linger."

"Ah, but I'm waiting for you. We're about to go on a tour of the house from foyer to attic."

"Indeed we are not."

"Very well, I shall go without you. That is, if you will trust me to go alone. Aren't you afraid I might pilfer a trinket or two to pawn when we get to London?"

"I am no longer surprised by anything you do, Mr. Harcourt."

If truth be told, Juliana wanted desperately to see the house. When she finally agreed to accompany him, she only half believed it was to keep him honest.

They started at the long stairway leading up from the kitchen into the corridor just off the wide entrance hall. Juliana had dared a single visit into the upstairs to place the note beneath the vase, but this time they delayed long enough to savor the beauty of the house and its furnishings.

Juliana had been in many country homes in her life. Some were like palaces with their delicately formal furnishings while others were decorated with rigorous attention to a theme. She remembered one such that belonged to Sir Edmund McReedy, who had built an elaborate replica of a Chinese pavilion complete with moon gate and koi pond.

But this house was different, and Juliana was drawn to it as if it had been built for her. Heavy, wide doors opened into the stone-floored foyer, which was a few steps down from the entrance. Marble pedestals, which she assumed normally held vases of flowers or potted ferns, graced each side of the door, and next to these were tall, narrow windows with brazed and leaded panes.

"See that chandelier?" Mr. Harcourt asked. "It dates back to the reign of Queen Elizabeth."

"How exquisite it must look when it's lighted. Heavens. I would venture to say it would take two hundred candles to fill it."

"More like three hundred."

She looked at him with curiosity. "I suppose you counted them?"

"Of course. Just what did you think I was doing while you were unpacking?"

"Believe me, Mr. Harcourt, I would be a fool to try to guess."

He gestured toward an open doorway through which appeared to be the salon or drawing room and offered his arm. "Shall we?"

She nodded, hardly noticing the rich tapestries that graced the walls near the oak staircase. His arm was firm against her fingers, and when he pulled her hand close against his side to guide her through the doorway, Juliana was sure she felt the thudding of his heart against his ribs. It was a heady sensation. One she wasn't at all prepared to deal with.

The furniture was shrouded in ghostly sheets of cotton material to keep it free of dust. Even so, there was a look of neglect about the room, and Juliana longed to throw back the burgundy velvet draperies and open the windows. The house was so still. Velvet rugs in shades of burgundy, teal and ivory dotted the oak floor and muffled their footsteps.

Mr. Harcourt patted her hand, then let it fall as he stepped to a table. "I'll light the lamp so that we can see. I'd open the draperies, but the windows are shuttered tight."

As the room sprang into light, Juliana folded her hands across her chest. "What a dreadful waste. This room should be alive with laughter." She lifted the corner of a cloth and examined a chair. "Just see this lovely silk. I'd venture that the owner hasn't even looked at it for a year or more. He probably has so much money he's forgotten about the place. I wonder what kind of man he is."

"Probably a lecherous old goat chasing after every demirep he can get his hands on, wouldn't you say?"

"Oh, I wouldn't go that far. He may be a perfect gentleman, for all I know. He certainly has fine taste." She walked over to a group of paintings hanging on the wall. One of them was an elderly man with a thick beard that nearly concealed his mouth, but there was something intriguing about his eyes. Juliana began to laugh.

"Given a few years, you are going to look just like him if you continue to let your beard grow."

"Indeed? You find his appearance funny?"

"Funny? A bird could nest in that beard, and he would never know it."

"But I thought you liked men with beards."

"Moustaches, not beards." She turned to look at him with sudden curiosity. "What made you think I like men with beards? I never told you so."

"Sometimes, Juliana, actions speak louder than words."

She scarcely noticed his use of her given name, because it occurred to her with a sinking feeling that she knew what he was trying to say. She looked up at him beseechingly, hoping that he would not be so cruel as to confront her with her own folly.

He put his hands on her shoulders and smiled down at her in his devilish way. "Yes, Juliana. It's true, isn't it? At first I thought it might have been a dream, you leaning over me, so close, so mystical that I couldn't tell where the moonlight ended and you began. And when your lips just barely touched mine..."

"Stop, please. Don't say any more." She put her hands to her face.

His eyes grew dark and unfathomable. "All right. I'll not bedevil you now, but one day, Mrs. Penridge, I'm going to repay in kind that favor you bestowed upon me while I was half-conscious."

CHAPTER THREE

JULIANA WAS BESIEGED by a tumult of conflicting emotions simply by the mere fact of standing near him. Mr. Harcourt was extremely appealing in a masculine sense. It had been a long time since a man, any man, had talked to her in such an unconventional way, and she felt dreadfully unnerved. She had always enjoyed being kissed, even if she had never particularly liked the more intimate aspects of love. Now, for the first time in her adult life, Juliana found herself wondering if it had just been Cedric that she had so thoroughly disliked.

As Mr. Harcourt's gaze lingered on hers, the twitch of his moustache sent shivers of anticipation down her spine. What could it matter if she let him kiss her? After all, they were alone. Who would ever know? The strength of her feelings made her tense, and she drew back.

"What is it, Juliana? Of what are you thinking?"

"I...my husband...I was thinking of him." It was a bending of the truth, but she could hardly share her fantasy. He stepped back as quickly as if she had struck him.

His voice was harsh. "Forgive me. It was not my wish to remind you of him. If you'll excuse me, I think I shall get some air."

It was well into the afternoon before he returned. When he did, he was drenched to the skin, but there was a little-boy look of adventure about him as he came into the kitchen.

"See what I've brought? Can you cook it, do you think?" He was holding up a dead hare.

"Of course I can, but wherever did you get it?"

"I snared it near the lake."

Juliana was shocked. "Mr. Harcourt, have you no idea what you've done? Poaching is punishable by death or at the very least, transportation."

He leaned indulgently against the doorframe. "I'll clean it, and while you're putting it into a pot, I'll find some dry clothes to put on."

She shook her head apprehensively. "You wouldn't take clothing belonging to the owner, would you?"

"Well, I certainly wouldn't pinch something belonging to the maids."

Juliana blushed, but apparently the double meaning didn't occur to him. At any rate, it was useless to argue. He was determined to make himself at home. And wouldn't it be lovely, just for once, to sit down to a proper meal? She was sick of porridge and soup made from barley and moldy vegetables from the root cellar. There were tins of flour in the pantry and enough supplies to make a sort of bread. She began to feel a sense of excitement building inside her.

She had never before cooked for a man. When Cedric was alive, there was the staff of servants to look after them. Later she could no longer afford to keep the servants, but by then Cedric was dead. But most of all, Juliana wanted to do something to please Mr. Harcourt.

When Juliana finally had the rabbit stewing in the pot along with savory herbs and onions, she paused to look around the kitchen where Mr. Harcourt was sipping a cup of tea. Gowns hung everywhere. She had to duck down to move from one end of the room to the other.

"They aren't drying very fast, are they?" she said.

"It takes time. The gowns were quite sodden."

She held her skirt out in front of her. "This old crepe has begun to feel like a uniform. I shall be glad to dispose of it when the time comes."

He raised his gaze toward the ceiling. "I pray that it will be soon. Egad. The kitchen looks like a whore's bedroom, with all the gowns hanging about."

Juliana was miffed. "Aye, and I suppose you'd be the one to know."

"Watch your tongue, my girl. I only meant that when one is as tall as I it isn't easy to move about. The drapings hardly add to the feeling of elegant dining."

"On which you are an authority, no doubt. This isn't Carlton House, and the venerable age of your hare would not qualify it as a feast for the Prince Regent, so let us have no more complaints over the surroundings."

He laughed. "Indeed. You have begun to sound like my wife."

The words struck like a knife through her heart. "Your wife? Y-you didn't tell me you were married."

"No, Juliana. I didn't." He smiled. "Don't look so stricken. The reason I didn't tell you about my wife is because I have none. I have never had time to take a wife."

She felt the color flow back into her face, and to cover her emotions she snapped at him. "Well, that comes as no great surprise. Whether or not you have managed to secure a wife is no concern of mine. Rather, my concern would necessarily be with the poor woman who had to put up with your inflated self-esteem."

He bowed outrageously and pretended to be contrite. "A thousand pardons, madam, for misjudging you. Now if you will excuse me, I intend to see what the master of the house has to offer in the way of a wardrobe for a man with my obvious lack of breeding."

Cocky. That's what he is, Juliana thought as she watched him saunter toward the door. He made an elaborate pretense of ducking under the gowns as he went. The laughter that drifted back when he was gone did little to soothe her temper, and yet for some reason Juliana found she was smiling.

Suddenly she had a thought. Earlier she had glimpsed a tiny intimate dining alcove at one end of the master's study upstairs. What would it matter if she set a table for the two of them there? The food could be sent up by dumbwaiter from the kitchen to the butler's pantry off the dining room. And while she was about it, why not borrow the family's everyday china instead of the heavy pewter used by the servants? The more she thought about it, the more it became an adventure.

Juliana found there was a definite chill to the study, but since a fire was laid in the grate, she decided it could do no harm to light the tinder. She had found a goodly supply of linens and a lovely set of yellow-sprigged china in the butler's pantry. Despite the cotton covers the table and chairs had a sifting of dust that appalled her. Discovering beeswax in the supply cabinet, she proceeded to polish them until they glowed with the rich patina of fine wood.

It was a man's room, comfortable with soft chairs, convenient lamps, and walls lined with books. The table in the alcove could serve equally as well for writing or dining.

When the table was set, Juliana stepped back to study it. The yellow linen cloth matched exactly the tiny flowers in the plates. She had found settings of silver in a flannel-lined drawer and had taken the time to polish them to a rich luster. The fire burning in the grate mellowed the persimmon and gold colors that accented the teal blue of the carpets and draperies in the study and cast flickering shadows across the room. Juliana added a pair of silver candlesticks and inserted tall candles, which had seen only a little use. Mr. Harcourt was sure to be impressed.

A quick look at the pot of stew assured her that it would not bubble over. Water was set to boil in the kettle, and all that remained was to toast the bread dough in the skillet. She would have liked to bake a sweet, but without eggs... Then she spied the preserved dates Mr. Harcourt had brought from the storeroom. Served with the walnuts she had found in a ginger jar in the cupboard, they would make a nice ending for their meal.

There was just time to freshen up before dinner. Hurrying back to the servants' wing, she threw open the door to her bedchamber and stopped. Lying on the bed was a lovely blue brocade gown, its full skirt spread out to reveal panels of delicate embroidery. Her breath caught in her throat. It was exquisite. The style was perhaps a bit out of fashion, but somehow that only added to the charm of the expensive gown.

But she couldn't wear it. It was out of the question. Regret was written on her face as she turned to the mirror and started to smooth her hair. The reflection was less than pleasing. On impulse Juliana held the blue gown up in front of her. It would fit almost perfectly. She was certain of it.

Oh, bother! She wanted so much to wear it. Poverty left so much to be desired. If her own gowns had been dry, she wouldn't have considered borrowing this even for a moment. Her own dresses were equally as charming. But she had been wearing the black crepe for days now, during all the time she had traveled, then trudging through the storm, and later supporting Miles Harcourt through the rain, then drawing water from the cistern and preparing their meals. No wonder it looked as if she were little more than a charwoman. Perhaps that was how Mr. Harcourt thought of her.

Before she had time to change her mind, she had washed and changed into the gown. It clung to her figure as if it were meant for her. Juliana's spirits bubbled as she faced the mirror. It wasn't exactly Gentleman's Night at Almack's Club, but she looked festive, indeed. On impulse she pulled the mobcap from her head and allowed her hair to flow free. It fell like a caress over her creamy shoulders where a rather bold expanse of skin showed above the neckline of the gown. Juliana considered unearthing her one remaining piece of jewelry, a necklace that had belonged to her mother, but she decided against it.

After all, she was still not entirely convinced that Miles Harcourt was not some kind of adventurer. He had admittedly just returned from the sea. He might pocket the necklace without any thought to her feelings. If she fought him, there was no telling what he might do.

Looking at the hint of exposed bosom above the ruffled neckline, she repeated the thought. Indeed, there was no telling what he might do, given the appropriate provocation. It might be prudent to offer less in the way of temptation. She rummaged in the drawer of the dresser she was using for the lace fichu she sometimes wore with her crepe. It would solve the problem quite nicely.

Twenty minutes later she was ready, but Mr. Harcourt had yet to make his appearance. The hare stew filled the kitchen with a delightful aroma. Time was when she would have turned up her nose at such a mundane dish, but hunger worked wonders for an appetite. She checked the buns in the skillet. The crusts had turned an amber brown, and she could all but taste them with a dribble of honey or the fine apricot jelly Miles had found in the larder.

Miles! She mentally chastised herself. It was imprudent for her to even be thinking of him by his given name. It was too easy to forget oneself and use it in front of him. True, he had on occasion called her Juliana, but since she had no fondness for the name Penridge, she had not wanted to object. It was too awkward to ask him to call her by her maiden name, and she would not dare admit to being a countess.

Be honest, she thought. *You like the way your name sounds on his tongue. In fact, there are many things you like about him.* She wrapped her arms around herself and stood there, her imagination running free.

"Are you chilled, Juliana? I was afraid the gown might not be warm enough, so I fetched a shawl." He stopped and stared at her.

For a moment Juliana thought a stranger had entered the room. He was dressed in fawn-colored breeches that molded his thighs and accented his trim waist. They were topped off with a ruffled silk blouse of the same shade and a brown whipcord jacket. But the greatest change was in his face. He had apparently found a razor and made short work of the coarse beard. All that remained was the enticing moustache, which brought a flood of color to her face when she remembered the feel of it against her lips.

Without taking his gaze from her, he walked across the room. "By all that is holy, you are a delight to the eyes."

She forced herself to meet his gaze. "Thank you. And thank you, too, for finding the gown for me to wear. We shouldn't, but somehow I feel suspended from reality in this place, and I find it hard to deal with guilt."

"Don't ever speak of guilt. If the owner of this gown could see you now, she would beg you to keep it, knowing she could never wear it again, considering how lovely it looks on you." He moved close and placed the shawl over her shoulders. "I see we're dining upstairs. It was kind of you to be so thoughtful." He smiled. "Or did you make the arrangements out of respect to the venerable age of the hare?"

She shot a look at him and lifted her chin. "No, indeed. I feared that your delicate stomach might rebel at the presence of the laundry hanging about. And no doubt you would have blamed it on my cooking ability."

"Touché. It appears that dinner is ready. May I help you to carry it to the dumbwaiter?"

"If you wish."

They were silent as they arranged the food in the lift, then walked upstairs to the master's study. Juliana was lost in thought. Their situation had suddenly taken on another dimension with the two of them dressed for dinner and their circumstances a distance removed from a question of need. It was almost as if they belonged here, as if they were man and wife, about to sit down to an early dinner. Was he thinking the same thoughts? She wouldn't put it past him to try to carry the fantasy a step farther. And if he did, what would she do? She was saved from answering to her conscience when she heard the pop of a champagne bottle.

"Mr. Harcourt, you didn't!"

"I'm afraid I did." He grinned. "There is a goodly supply of wine in the cellar below the house. I'm sure one small bottle, or even two, would not be missed. In any case, it can't be recorked, so we might as well enjoy it. Can you find some glasses?"

She nodded, then hurried down the corridor to the butler's pantry. A moment later she returned with two crystal goblets and held them while he poured. He lifted his glass and touched it to hers.

"To what shall we drink?"

"I . . . to our host, of course."

"Um . . . let's say to our host and to the lady who brings laughter to his lips."

She smiled. "Yes, I like that." They touched glasses and sipped, all the while never taking their gaze from each other. Finally Juliana was forced to look away because she felt a sudden surge of emotion. "I . . . I think perhaps we ought to sit down, Mr. Harcourt. The stew will be getting cold."

He held her chair, then seated himself. For a moment he sat there, contemplating her with great intensity. Then he spoke.

"Would it be asking too much for you to call me Miles? Given our circumstances, it seems foolish for you to call me Mr. Harcourt."

"Very well, if that is what you want. But only for tonight."

"Good. That calls for another glass of champagne."

"Just a small one, please. I am not used to spirits, and I am not certain they agree with me."

He stroked his chin. "It might be interesting to find out."

She raised an eyebrow. "Indeed? You are wasting your time if you think even champagne will make me amenable to seeing things your way."

"Seeing things my way? Just what things did you mean, Juliana?"

Her tone was dry. "I was referring to your penchant for taking over this house."

"Oh, that. I was hoping that your mind was on more interesting pursuits. Well, never mind. We shall see what transpires. In the meantime, I should like very much to sample the stew."

They ate slowly, as if to enjoy each morsel to the fullest. For Juliana, at least, there was more pleasure in sitting across the table from this handsome rake than could possibly be derived from the food. She was grateful she had yielded to temptation and worn the borrowed gown, for undoubtedly, this had to be one of the happiest moments of her life. In spite of their almost constant verbal battle, Juliana knew that deeper, more tumultuous feelings lay just below the surface of their words.

Finally, when they were nearly finished, Miles poured another glass of champagne. He pushed his chair back from the table with the look of a satisfied man. "Truly, Juliana, the hare must not have been as old as you tried to make me believe, for it was so tender it seemed to melt in my mouth."

"Only because I laced it with herbs and pounded it to the thinness of paper. After which I simmered it for two full hours. I must admit that despite the creature's age it made an elegant stew, and I do thank you for your trouble.''

He raised an eyebrow. ''Egad. Has the champagne mellowed you that much? We must celebrate with a waltz.''

She laughed. ''Silly. We have no music.''

''Don't be such a doubter.'' He got up and strode toward a glass case that was partially concealed by a cotton sheet. Opening the case, he extracted a small square box and brought it to the table. Then he went to her chair and offered his arm. ''Shall we?''

She hesitated but decided to go along with his game. Rising from the chair, Juliana placed her hand on his arm as he reached down and lifted the lid of the music box. It opened to reveal a carved replica of two people spinning around in each other's arms while at the same time being caught up in a very romantic kiss to the tinkling strains of *Lavender Lace*.

Miles's hand centered on her back as she placed her hand in his warm palm. He was an expert dancer. Juliana had little experience with the new dance, called the *waltz*, but it seemed to be a simple step, and she had no trouble following him.

They whirled about the room, taking care to avoid the furniture and the rugs, which were scattered about the floor. Juliana was beginning to feel quite giddy, but she knew the champagne had nothing to do with it. No spirits could equal the heady sensation that flooded her veins when Miles looked at her or touched her. His hands communicated a strength that drew her like a moth to a flame, and she wanted to move into his arms and rest her face against that broad shoulder. But he held her at a respectable distance. Was it the style of the dance, or had he no wish for closer contact? She felt a vague disappointment.

As the spring on the music box began to wind down, the music became slower and slower until they were barely moving across the floor. Miles held her away from him and studied her face.

"Juliana," he whispered. "You are so beautiful I sometimes think I died out there in the storm and was rescued by an angel."

She recognized the intensity of his voice and knew that she must soon break the spell.

The music had tinkled to a stop, but Miles continued to hold her in his arms. It seemed as if each of Juliana's senses was attuned to his very existence. The fresh, soapy scent of his skin, pinkened now where the blade had scraped away his beard, the pull of his shoulder muscles against her hand, the compelling gaze of his wide-set cobalt blue eyes as they locked with hers, all served to quicken her pulse.

He lowered his head, his breath fluttering against her cheek like the touch of a kitten's paw. "Juliana, my sweet. How truly desirable you are. The royal court with its parade of beauties of noble birth could not equal your loveliness."

She felt drugged with happiness, and she laughed deep in her throat. "You flatter me, Miles. I fear the wine has gone to your head."

He shook his head. "It is not the wine, my dear, but being here alone, so completely alone with you. One might come to believe that the real world has even ceased to exist."

"Could it be that the two of us are all that is left of this civilization?" she teased.

He nodded. "And what would you say to that?"

She drew back, knowing what he wanted to hear but unwilling to voice the words. Instead she smiled. "I would say that you had best not chance to break your leg, Mr. Harcourt, because I have no knowledge of the surgeon's art."

His gaze narrowed and flickered with deviltry. "And could you serve as your own midwife, Juliana? If not, you had best learn the skill for I warrant this: if we were left alone, it would be a scant nine months before you would indeed have need of it."

Juliana felt the heat rise in her face, and she found it necessary to lighten the mood. "Oh, yes, I do seem to recall your boast that you had the strength of ten men."

"That may have been a slight exaggeration, but in the bedchamber I could summon the strength of a dozen... That is, if I were given the right partner."

She felt a moment of panic. "Then you had best look elsewhere, Mr. Harcourt, for I fear I do not qualify."

"Indeed? I think I am the best judge of that."

Juliana stiffened. "This has gone far enough, Mr. Harcourt. We must not continue to flaunt convention."

He closed his eyes for an instant, and once again she was entranced by the thickness of his lashes. But then he drew away.

"All right, Mrs. Penridge. Your wish is my command."

She forced a smile and inclined her head in a fine imitation of Princess Caroline. "Very good. Suppose you behave like a proper lackey and help me carry the dishes to the dumbwaiter."

He made a face, then bowed. "I am ever your faithful servant, ma'am."

Juliana just barely managed to hide her smile. One thing she knew for sure. Miles Harcourt would never consent to be anyone's lackey for very long.

CHAPTER FOUR

MILES ACCOMPANIED her downstairs to the kitchen where they proceeded to unload the dumbwaiter. He was unusually pensive, and Juliana began to wonder if he were angry, but then he spoke with marked intensity.

"We may not yet be alone on this earth, my sweet Juliana, but it doesn't matter, for we can pretend we are. This house can be ours for a month, or even two, and who is to know the difference?"

Juliana pulled back, as if he had slapped her. "Don't even think such an indecent thing. Is it then your impression that I am nothing but a trollop, a demirep who is good for a month or two until you have tired of her? If you have no respect for our absent landlord, you must at least have consideration for me."

"I didn't mean to..."

"But of course you did. What else could you possibly have meant? You certainly weren't asking for my hand in marriage."

He stroked his chin. "If I had been, would you have accepted?"

He caught her by surprise, and she was unprepared to answer. It shouldn't have required a decision. Dear

heaven, she had only known the man a few days.
Truthfully, she didn't know him at all because he had
yet to impart anything to her but the most superficial
information about his own affairs. Still, the thought
of marriage to this man had a way of unsettling her.

"You haven't answered, Juliana. Would you accept if I asked you to be my wife?"

She moved away from him. "Don't be absurd. The
question does not deserve an answer. I think the
champagne has gone to both our heads."

"Very well. Have it your own way. But one thing I
know for certain. You don't always speak the truth,
Juliana. You know as well as I do that we could have
enjoyed a lovely two months here at this country estate."

"I really would be most grateful, Miles, if you did
not refer to it again. And now, if you'll excuse me, I'll
see to redding up the kitchen."

She expected him to have the decency to allow her a
few minutes alone while she collected her wits, but he
insisted on helping her. All the while, his face held
absurd traces of amusement that made her wonder if
she were the cause of his high good humor.

At least he had not become abusive when she turned
aside his advances. Cedric would have considered her
refusal a personal insult and would doubtless have re-
sorted to force to have his way with her. The more she
saw of Miles Harcourt, the more surprised she was by
his ways. Indeed, if he truly had asked her to marry
him, would she have been tempted to say yes? She
pushed the thought aside. It was foolish to torment

herself with such thoughts. He had spoken in jest. That was all it was meant to be.

The hour was late by the time she finished setting the kitchen and scullery to rights. Miles had been a considerable help, but it was plain to see he was not in his element as a domestic. Once or twice she caught him watching her with obvious speculation. What was he thinking? The unasked question brought a rush of color to her face, which he was quick to notice.

"You blush easily, madam. What exotic thoughts run through your pretty head?"

She pretended anger. "I am not the one who must account for my thoughts, Mr. Harcourt. The pensive looks you have cast my way tonight would be enough to addle a saint."

"Ah, but you are no saint. Neither are you still a young maiden..." He laughed. "Of course, at present I have only your word for that."

"And that is all you shall have, Mr. Harcourt. As for the other, I don't pretend to be an innocent schoolgirl, but I strongly believe in decency and modesty. In the few hours we remain together, I expect you to control your baser impulses." She whisked off the apron she had used to cover her dress and hung it on a peg. "Now if you will excuse me, I would like to retire. Good night and thank you for a pleasant dinner, Mr. Harcourt," she said.

"The pleasure was mine, Juliana." He smiled, apparently unmoved by their verbal skirmishes.

She studied his face then shook her head in bewilderment. "Miles, I simply don't understand you. Half the time I can't tell whether you are speaking seriously or in jest.''

"But hasn't it been said that many a truth could be found 'neath the disguise of a jest?'' He put his hands on her shoulders and locked his gaze with hers and his voice took on an unexpected tenderness.

"Do not concern yourself, Juliana. You are quite safe with me. I plan to spend the night in the master's suite. After all, I share his clothing, so why not his bed?''

"You are indeed hopeless, Miles, but I know how useless it is to beg you to be considerate.''

"Of whom? You? I thought it most considerate of me to allow you to lie unmolested in your virginal bedchamber.''

"I was speaking of our landlord, as you well know. Good night, Miles.'' She moved quickly away from his touch and hurried to the door. At the last minute she turned, smiling. "And yes. It is most considerate of you to respect my wishes.'' Before he could respond, she fled down the corridor toward the servants' stairs.

By the time she reached the bedroom, she was breathless. Even as she closed the door after her, she wondered why it had seemed so important to hurry. One look in the mirror left no doubt in her mind. She was running away from her own feelings. If she had stayed a minute longer, he might have taken her in his arms, and she knew too well what temptation lay in that direction.

Sailor, rogue, adventurer? Whatever the man might be, Miles Harcourt had a way with him that could set fire to her blood as no other man ever could. Perhaps it was only the present state of her circumstances that made her so vulnerable. She leaned against the closed door as she tried to catch her breath. She had been alone before. Cedric was dead by another's hand, but he had left her alone often enough in the past when he had chosen a warmer bed than she could ever offer him.

After his death, the men of her acquaintance considered her fair game, and though they paid her court, their intentions were far from honorable, and she ignored them. It mattered little. There was none who appealed to her...until now. This time, being alone was different. She moved to the chest and studied herself in the hazy mirror.

"Woman, you're truly daft," she whispered aloud. "Miles Harcourt is at best an adventurer. If he doesn't already know you're nobility, he certainly suspects. He as much as said so." She smiled wryly. Not that it mattered one whit. Her title was meaningless without the funds to go with it. Still, there were unprincipled men of low birth who would give a great deal to be able to boast of having bedded a lady.

She stared wide-eyed at her reflection. It had been months since her face had so much color. Was she feverish? Could she have caught a chill? She touched her face, then laughed helplessly. If indeed this was a fever, it was a fever of the blood. She was going to have to be very careful where Miles Harcourt was concerned. The sooner she took herself to London, the better off she would be.

It was noon the following day before her gowns were dry enough to fold. Fortunately there was little damage. Only three or four of the velvets would need to be steamed to restore their vibrant colors. One pair of satin slippers had to be discarded, but several more attractive pairs remained. They would surely see her through until she was able to find suitable employment.

Miles was most cheerful and tactful when he came downstairs about a half hour after Juliana went down to prepare breakfast. She carefully suggested that they begin to make plans to leave for London on the following day. He simply nodded and smiled but made no comment. After he finished his scones and jelly, he told her he was going out and would return later.

She busied herself about the house in an effort to set things right. As careful as she had been, there were still obvious signs that the house had been recently occupied. By late afternoon her trunk was repacked, and her black crepe was washed and pressed. It had taken a tremendous amount of willpower to again don the hated black crepe de chine. Miles was right. It was hypocritical. Still, it was a form of protection. Black, particularly mourner's black, commanded a certain amount of respect. It also served to remind her to preserve what little dignity she had left.

Miles appeared a short time later at the kitchen door with a creel packed with several fish. Juliana clapped her hands together. "Oh, where did you find those beauties? They look marvelously fresh."

His expression was wry. "It was nothing. They just happened to be marching along the verge, and I ..."

"Oh, do be serious! You caught them in the lake, didn't you?"

"The lady's a bloomin' genius." He slapped his forehead with his hand.

"Stop it, Miles. I just wondered where you found a pole and everything."

"I pinched one from the shed, of course. The old goat who owns this place has a bit of everything stashed away out there."

"You put it back, of course."

"Of course."

She studied his face, a worried frown creasing her brow. "Miles, we will leave tomorrow, won't we? For London, I mean."

"Just how do you propose to get there? Walk?"

"Surely we can beg a ride with someone...a farmer, perhaps? Farmers make trips to market to sell their goods."

"Aye, but rarely so far as London. It's a good two days' trip."

"Then we shall have to stop midway and find another ride. I have a few extra coins left but not enough to spare. Besides, I must be cautious, or I'll have little left to pay for lodgings until I can find a position."

"Juliana, my sweet." His voice was infinitely patient. "Do you have any idea how far it is to the next farm? The roads are still muddy from the storm. You would be mired down before you'd gone a mile. We will just have to remain here until it dries up a bit, and then we'll see what we can do about getting to London."

Tears began to form at the back of her eyes. "But we can't stay here indefinitely."

"I don't intend to, but a few days more can do no harm."

She looked at him, grateful that he couldn't read her thoughts. No harm, indeed! Was the man blind and insensitive? Was he oblivious of how she responded to him? No. He wasn't that blind. But if not, then it was conceivable he meant to take advantage of her. She felt a tear slide down her cheek, and he started to touch it with his thumb but dropped his hands.

"I...the fish. My hands reek from the stench." He looked helpless. "I would take you to London sooner if I could, Juliana, but these things take time. Do you find my company so utterly distasteful?"

"It isn't that, as you well know, even though there are times when I find your behavior most insufferable."

He grinned. "At least I consider it a shade better than distasteful." He picked up the creel and tucked it under his arm. "I'll clean these fellows and trust them to your tender mercies in the kitchen. Dinner again in the study?"

"I . . . yes. If you wish."

"I do. I found it quite pleasant last night."

"Then will you promise not to steal another bottle of champagne?"

"I give you my word of honor, Juliana. I've no need of champagne to lighten my spirits. Not when I have you sitting across the table from me."

Juliana smiled. "Be serious, Miles."

"When you smile like that you make even your widow's weeds look enchanting." He leaned against the doorjamb as he studied her face. "Tell me, Juliana. What makes you happy?"

She shot him a surprised look. "What a strange question. Many things, of course. I'd have to think about it."

He had been right when he said she wasn't completely honest. But how could she tell him that she had never been happier than she was right now? The time she had spent alone with him was like a fragment of a dream. She dreaded the thought of waking to find him gone.

Juliana wanted to turn the question around and ask what made him happy, but she was afraid his answer might hurt too much. It was impossible to imagine that he, too, could find such unbelievable happiness here alone with her. Instead she made light of it, as she had learned to do when things became serious.

The rest of the day and evening passed pleasantly, and though Juliana frequently noticed that Miles was studying her face when she was supposedly unaware, he made no overtures toward her, and she was grateful. Another day passed, and then two more. Days filled with sunshine and youthful frolics on the rocky shore of the lake. Miles found a boat upended in a boathouse and rowed them out into the middle of the lake where he fished and she enjoyed being in the sun. He gathered snowdrops and wove them into a crown while she picked winter mushrooms for their dinner.

One morning the two of them roamed through the house, exploring nooks and crannies. Juliana discovered a rag doll with odious red hair and one black button eye. The other must have been lost long ago since there was no spot marking its former location. There was something pathetic about the doll that warmed Juliana's heart, and she hugged it close.

Miles shook his head. "Egad, she's ugly. She reminds me of a teacher I once had."

"I think I'll call her Mrs. Frobisher. She looks stern enough to be a chaperon."

"For once we agree. Here's a Dresden doll. Why don't you trade. The rag doll has no value whatsoever."

She patted it affectionately. "What does it matter? The true value is to the one who holds it, and I think Mrs. Frobisher is absolutely divine. Much nicer than those cold porcelain dolls with their painted smiles."

He looked highly amused. "I'll venture to guess that you also rescue stray cats as well as sailors who have been set upon by thugs."

"I don't make a habit of it," she said, gently resting her chin on the doll she was holding to her shoulder.

He doffed an imaginary hat and swept into a low bow. "Then I am most grateful that you made an exception in my case, Lady Juliana, for I truly owe my life to you."

She sucked in her breath, shaken by his use of her title. Had he discovered the fact that she was a countess? Her voice shook. "Indeed? And why have we become so formal?"

"Because it is less difficult to say certain things when we follow the rules of Polite Society."

She felt something inside her curl into a knot. "What is it, Miles? What are you trying to say? Has something happened?"

"It's nothing, Juliana, my sweet, and yet everything."

He was obviously stricken about something. His eyes were dark with emotion. She stared at him wide-eyed, scarcely able to breathe as he continued.

"I have pondered this all day and wondered how to tell you. Although it pains me, I fear it is time we make ourselves ready to go to London on the morrow."

She lowered her eyes, afraid to let him see the tears that sprang unbidden to her lashes. "I see." She laughed without humor. "Strange, isn't it, that it is you, not I, who has made the final decision. I fear, Miles, that I have come to love this place with its wide verandas, the woods, the lake, the sweet smell of country-fresh air."

He took her hand and pressed his lips to it and held it there for a moment. "You could stay, of course, but I would miss seeing you every day."

"And I you, Miles, despite your dreadful behavior."

He saw that she was smiling through her tears, and he pulled her close against him.

Juliana allowed herself the luxury of a few brief moments in his arms, knowing full well that she could never permit it to happen again. Then she forced a smile and pulled away.

"Well, then. There is much to do to set the house to rights before we are ready to leave. Have you thought of how we are going to travel?"

"I have a few ideas."

"Miles . . ." Juliana hesitated. "I must confess, I haven't been quite honest with you. I have a few coins that could help pay for the rental of a cart and horse."

"As a matter of fact, I also have a little money tucked away."

Juliana grinned. "Did you think I might steal it from you? Where did you have it hidden? I didn't find it when I washed your clothing."

"Suffice it to say that I hid it well. When a man wakes up in a strange bed with a strange woman standing over him, he is well advised to take precautions."

"Yes, well, you would know about those things, I'm sure. Now, as to our transportation?"

"I think I might be able to rent a carriage from one of the neighboring farmers. While you are taking care of things here, I'll walk down the lane and see what I can find."

Juliana went upstairs to get the money she had promised to contribute. At the last minute he tried to refuse, but Juliana was adamant.

"I insist you take it, Miles. After all, were it not for me and my trunks, you could easily make do with a saddle horse."

He finally gave in and took the money from her. A short time later he left. Juliana stood at the gate as he strode down the lane toward the country road. He turned once and waved to her, and she had a fleeting panic that she would never see him again. It took all of her self-control not to call after him, to beg him to come back to take her with him.

She admonished herself to stop behaving like a child. There were linens to wash, floors to scrub, tables to polish. Juliana was determined to leave the house looking better than when she had arrived.

Miles was gone for a very long time. Twelve o'clock passed and then one, then two. Juliana had been unable to eat. The very thought of being without him stuck in her throat, threatening to make her ill. What if he never came back?

She paused, her feather duster stopped in midair. Wouldn't it be like him, though, just to disappear into thin air as if he had never been here? He had no luggage to return for. He had arrived here with nothing but the clothes on his back and the odd bit of money he had been able to hide in his smallclothes. Now he had a full belly and clean clothes, thanks to the complete wardrobe left behind by the master of the house. And her money!

She slapped the duster against the edge of the table, sending dust flying in all directions. *The swine!* How could he do this to her? It wasn't just the money, though heaven knew she needed it desperately. And it wasn't just the thought of being alone. These past few days had introduced a new perspective into her life. They had taught her the difference between being alone and being lonely. While she was married to Cedric, she cherished the hours when he was away. But it was different with Miles. He was gone, and she knew now what it was like to feel empty inside.

Darkness fell, and her anger gave way to tears. One moment she hated him for having ever come into her life. The next moment she admitted to herself that she wouldn't have missed this bittersweet experience for anything in the world.

"Life isn't easy," her father had once told her, "but we must take what it offers and learn from it."

Well, she had learned her lesson this time. Before she put her trust in a man, any man, she was going to make sure and certain that she was fully able to stand on her own.

"A pox on you, Miles Harcourt!" she declared, banking the fire in the kitchen fireplace. It was seconds later that she heard the rhythmic clop of horses coming up the lane.

She ran to the window. "A carriage!" Could it be Miles? Or was it the absentee owner come to have her arrested? She was too petrified to move until she saw Miles open the door and jump down. He ran to the service door, and she heard him coming toward her down the steps to the kitchen.

Julian dabbed at her eyes, hoping against hope that the redness didn't show as he flung open the door. She turned to face him, and his face was split by a grin.

"So you've seen, then? I've found us a carriage and a driver to take us all the way to London." He saw the look on her face, and he went toward her. "What is it, lass? What's wrong? You look as if you've seen a ghost."

She shook her head. "It's nothing. I'm glad you're back, that's all."

"Ho, ho! So that's what this is all about. You thought I'd run off on you."

"Don't be ridiculous. I know you'd never do that until you'd got the rest of my money."

It was obvious to both of them that she was lying, but it was the best she could do without yielding to the temptation to run to him and smother him with kisses.

He laughed. "Indeed. A man has to make a crust however he can."

"You were gone so long, Miles."

"Aye. These are difficult times for the farmers. It took some hard bargaining to find a man who was willing to part with horses, not knowing where to find another pair so cheap. Mister Carruthers, lucky for us, was hoping to go to London to find work now that the cottage industries are shutting down. So now we have a driver as well as horses."

"You've done well, Miles," Juliana said, tears hiding just below the surface.

"The carriage is old, and we can't afford outriders to accompany us. So to be safe, we'll have to travel during the daytime."

"Then we shall see more of the countryside." She tucked her hands beneath her shawl. "You must be starved. Have you eaten?"

"Several hours ago, but no need to bother. The farmer who sold us the carriage sent along a hamper of pork pasties, cheese, and bread hot from the oven."

Juliana blinked back the tears from her eyes, but she couldn't keep the sound of them from her voice. "It . . . it s-sounds wonderful."

He reached for her hands. "You're crying. You did think I had run out on you, didn't you?"

Juliana jerked away. "That's utter rubbish. I am merely distressed because you hate my cooking so much you had to bribe another woman to do it for us.''

He grinned. ''There will be plenty of time for you to practice later on when my stomach has had a chance to recover.''

Juliana's eyes flew open. ''Miles Harcourt, you are despicable!''

''So I've been told.'' His smile took the sting from his words, and she had to turn quickly to hide her own.

CHAPTER FIVE

THE CARRIAGE RUMBLED through the countryside at a steady clip despite the poorly matched pair of strawberry roans. Juliana rested her head against the musty cushion and closed her eyes. It had been harder than she had expected to leave the warm sanctuary of the country house. Although the landscape had yet to feel even the very first awakenings of spring, she could sense the waiting: the primal instincts of buds about to burst into bloom.

Her eyelids fluttered open as she felt Miles's gaze upon her. An amused smile flickered around his eyes, and she became unsettled. "What is it, Miles? Have I a bit of pigeon pie or apricot tart on my face?"

"No. I was just thinking about my mother and how surprised she will be when we reach the house."

"I've no doubt of that, and I must confess, I'm a bit unnerved about arriving unannounced. I would feel ever so much more comfortable staying at a public lodging house until I find employment and am able to pay for a flat."

"Nonsense. Mother is a bit reserved, but she will welcome you as our guest for as long as it takes you to find suitable employment and a place to live."

"You are certain there will be room for me at your home?"

He adjusted the sleeve of his coat and leaned his elbow against the plush-covered armrest. "I give you my word, Juliana. Have I disappointed you so far?" His smile was quizzical.

She had to admit that he had been most competent in finding them transport as well as arranging for a decent room last night at the dreadfully overcrowded Inn of the Golden Harp. Juliana had been appalled when the coach had passed through the porte cochere and she had seen the line of coaches and the phaetons and carriages waiting to be tended to by the harassed hostlers. The innkeeper had taken one look at Miles and had said there was not one room available, not to mention two.

"My good man," Miles had said, putting his hand on the innkeeper's shoulder and leading him a short distance away, just out of earshot. They had spoken for less than a minute when Miles returned.

"It's all arranged, Juliana. The innkeeper will see that a room is made ready." Before she could protest, he raised his hands. "As for myself, I shall share accommodations with another traveler."

"But it is so crowded. How did you ever manage it, Mr. Harcourt?"

He grinned, obviously aware that now that they had left the country house, Juliana saw fit to revert to more formal address. "It was simple. I told him that I'm of the nobility on my way to London to see the Prince Regent."

Juliana gasped. "You didn't! Truthfully, Mr. Harcourt. What did you tell him? I know you could never make him swallow a yarn like that."

"It was the best story I could think of at the time." He reached for her hand. "If you'd care to alight, I'll assist you to your room."

They were suddenly surrounded by lackeys who seemed almost to materialize from the daub-and-wattle walls of the Golden Harp. Miles gave orders that the horses be groomed and fed while he refreshed himself and ate supper.

Juliana's room was little more than a space under the eaves, but it was clean and comfortable. She had barely divested herself of her traveling cloak when a knock sounded at the door of her bedchamber. Thinking it must be Miles, Juliana frowned. A second thought assured her that Miles would never knock so timidly.

"Who is it?" she asked.

"Madam, forgive me. My name is Nadina Beaurivage." The young woman spoke with a slight French accent. "I would speak with you for a moment, if you would be so kind."

Juliana hesitated, then opened the door a crack. "Yes, what is it?"

"Please, may I come in? I am desperately in need of a position. The innkeeper's woman told me that you are traveling with a nobleman and that you are without benefit of a lady's maid."

Juliana opened the door to the woman who appeared to be a few years younger than herself. "Come in. I'm so sorry, Miss Beaurivage, but I fear you've been misled. I am going to London to look for work, and since I am without funds myself, there is no way that I can offer you help of any kind."

"*Oui*. I understand. I was hoping that I could accompany you to London. This—" she spread her hands "—this place is *très barbare*. So barbaric. I fear I shall die if I am forced to remain here another day. I am sorry to have bothered you, madam." She started to leave, but Juliana touched her arm.

"Wait, please. If it is simply transportation to London that you require, perhaps I can be of assistance. There are but two of us sharing the coach. I'm sure there would be room for another passenger."

"Oh, madam. Do you mean it? I would ever be your grateful servant."

"Nonsense. It's settled. But you must be ready to leave at first light. Mr. Harcourt would not delay long for either of us, I fear."

The young woman's luminous brown eyes moved wistfully toward the bed. Juliana sighed. "And I suppose you have no place to sleep tonight?"

"If madam would permit, I could sleep in the traveling coach."

"You would catch your death of cold in this damp weather. Here, there are several quilts. You can make a pallet on the floor against the wall."

Nadina's face blossomed with pleasure. "*Merci*, thank you, and in the morning I shall assist you with your toilette."

Despite the confines of the narrow bed, which was padded with only a thin mat of straw, Juliana slept soundly. When she awoke the next morning, Nadina was already washed and combed and had fetched hot water for Juliana's ablutions.

It had been many months since Juliana had had someone to look after her personal needs. She was well able to care for herself, but it was a pleasure to feel pampered once again.

Miles looked altogether rested and ready for anything when he knocked at her door. Juliana stepped into the corridor and quickly closed the door behind her so that he had no opportunity to see the room.

He looked surprised. "I didn't expect to be invited inside, Mrs. Penridge, but there was no need to slam the door so sharply."

"I—I'm sorry. The truth is, I have company." He looked shocked, but before he could say anything, she lifted her chin. "Mr. Harcourt, do be sensible and spare me your clever remarks. I have taken the liberty of inviting a young woman to join us en route to London."

"God's blood, woman. Have you taken leave of your senses?"

Juliana leveled her gaze at him. "Oh, don't look so appalled. The woman is harmless, I assure you. She is destitute and completely without protection. Since we have ample room in the carriage. I saw no reason not to share it with her."

Miles face reddened. "You might have had the good grace to consult with me first."

"I was certain of your generosity. Besides, my own money paid for a portion of this trip."

"Juliana, have you no idea what kind of people inhabit these roadside inns? She could be a cutpurse or a light-skirt or at the very least, an adventuress. It's only by the grace of God she didn't slit your throat during the night."

"She's soft-spoken and quite harmless; I'd venture my life on it."

"The answer is no, Juliana. Why, she might even be planning to meet up with highwaymen a few miles into the country. I absolutely will not risk our lives for the sake of charity."

Juliana folded her arms across her breast. "Then you must be the one to tell her."

"Indeed. I'll do so at once, with pleasure."

Juliana opened the door to her room. "Nadina? Would you come here, please?"

"*Oui*, madam. What is it?"

"This is Miles Harcourt. The man who is escorting me to London. He would like to speak with you."

"*Oui*, Monsieur Harcourt?" Nadina looked up at Miles with intensely brown eyes fringed with dark lashes, liquid brown eyes that were filled with trust and undisguised admiration. As he stared down at her, his mouth slightly open, she dropped a graceful curtsy, unconsciously accentuating her youthful curves.

He cleared his throat and inclined his head. "Ah, uh, Miss, uh."

"Beaurivage," she prompted.

"Yes, uh, Mrs. Penridge tells me that you wish to accompany us to London."

"*Oui, monsieur*. I would be most grateful, but I must be honest. I fear I have no money to pay my way. If madam would permit, I would be pleased to serve as her abigail."

He glanced at Juliana, then, out of embarrassment, he looked away. "In that case I see no reason why you should not accompany us. We shall leave directly after we dine."

"*Merci*. I shall be ever grateful, *monsieur*." Before he could stop her, she bent and kissed his hand. "If madam would permit, I will finish packing while you have breakfast."

Juliana found it difficult to keep a straight face as they walked downstairs. "You do have a way with people, Mr. Harcourt. You set her down so cleverly that I doubt she knows you refused her request."

"Mrs. Penridge. I told you once before that I don't take well to the needle."

"Tell me, Mr. Harcourt. If Nadina had been hatchet-faced and bent as an old crone, would you have been less subtle in your handling of the situation?"

He tucked her hand in his arm and escorted her toward the dining room. "I was only thinking of you, Mrs. Penridge. You could well use an accomplished abigail for a change."

Her voice took on a decided edge. "I beg your pardon. Are you telling me that I look unkempt?"

"Please, keep your voice down. Shrillness does not appeal to one's senses."

Juliana lowered her voice to a spitting whisper. "Neither does the sight of an old man ogling a young girl."

"Old man, you say? Why, Mrs. Penridge. I'm only a few years your senior. Surely you don't consider yourself old?"

"I'm old enough to know a lecherous look when I see one."

"My dear Mrs. Penridge, I do believe you are jealous of that child."

Juliana shot him a look. "Jealous? Don't be absurd. You may recall that it was I who insisted you keep your distance these past few days. I was only thinking of how defenseless the girl would be in the hands of an unprincipled seaman such as yourself."

He stroked his chin. "Now that you mention it, she does have a certain appeal. Perhaps the ride to London may be a bit more entertaining than our previous day's travel."

Juliana saw the twinkle in his eyes but was hard put to know whether to take him seriously or accept the fact that he was toying with her for his own amusement. She pulled her shawl around her and refused to rise to the bait.

Within the hour they were ready to travel. Juliana had packed some cheeses and bread along with a flask of tea for them to share in the carriage. Nadina ate a bit of cheese and bread and settled back in the corner of the carriage. Miles wasn't about to let her off easily.

"*Mademoiselle*, if I may be so bold. How is it that you happen to be alone and without funds in such an out-of-the-way place as the Inn of the Golden Harp?"

She laced her fingers together on her lap and sat up prim and straight. "Until a few days ago I served as lady's maid to the Baroness von Holten who was traveling with the baron to their house in the north country."

Nadina looked down at her hands. "Suddenly, without warning of any kind, I was discharged. For several days I lived at the inn with the hope of finding employment with some family who was passing through. But alas, my money ran out and the innkeeper threatened to evict me or, worse still, have me arrested."

Miles's face was set. "You stole money from the baroness? Was that why she discharged you?"

Juliana was shocked. "Mr. Harcourt! How can you be so insensitive?"

"No, *monsieur*. It was not that way at all." Nadina's face turned bright pink, and she looked away. "I am shamed to say this, but I must. The baroness discovered that the baron was making advances to me. It was not enough that I refused him. She no longer wanted me around as a temptation to her husband."

Miles spoke grudgingly. "Yes, I suppose that's possible."

Juliana all but snorted. "A pity, isn't it, that men are so unprincipled as to behave like animals around a pretty young girl."

Miles reached across to pat her hand, as if she were an old woman in her dotage who needed to be placated. "Indeed, Mrs. Penridge. How grateful you must be now that you no longer have to deal with such injustices."

Nadina saw the shocked expression on Juliana's face and leaned forward. "Oh, but *monsieur*, madam is one of the most beautiful women I have ever seen, for her age."

Miles burst into laughter.

"What is it? What have I said?" Nadina begged, bewilderment clouding her lovely eyes.

Juliana spread her hands. "Don't be disturbed, Nadina. Mr. Harcourt has all the sensitivity of—of a pig standing up to its shoulders in swill."

Miles started to say something, but Juliana silenced him with a look. For a while they each settled back into their respective places, content to doze or gaze from the square window at the passing countryside. The hours passed pleasantly.

They were just a short distance from London when Juliana finally closed her eyes and began thinking about what had transpired last night when they had arrived at the inn.

She was still hard put to understand the courteous way they had been treated. Upon their departure, the innkeeper had even gone so far as to be at the door to wish them a safe trip to London. Had Miles really claimed to be of the noble class? True, he had the bearing for it, but his countrified clothing and sun-darkened skin gave evidence to the fact that he was no follower of the haute monde.

The rasp of the iron-rimmed coach wheels against cobblestone brought her back to her present surroundings, and she leaned forward to peer out the window.

"Dear heaven, Mr. Harcourt. Has our driver taken a wrong turn? We seem to be in a very exclusive area."

"Have no fear, Mrs. Penridge. The driver is quite familiar with London. This is the Berkeley Square. Our destination is just a short distance after we make the turn onto Mount Street."

Juliana tried to see beneath his smooth facade, but his face betrayed nothing but confidence. Her heart began to pound. She found it difficult to draw a deep breath because of the constriction in her chest. Then slowly, one by one, the pieces began to fit together like the corridors to a maze. He had tricked her. That's what. Made her look the fool.

She glanced over at Nadina, who was sound asleep. "Mr. Harcourt," Juliana demanded quietly, "isn't it time you told me exactly where we are going and precisely who you are?"

He uncrossed his top boots and leaned forward. "I'm going home, Mrs. Penridge. And you are going with me."

She started to say something more when the carriage began to slow down in front of an ivy-covered stone wall that bordered a three-storey red-brick mansion. It was graced at the front by leaded windows and tall white pillars that rose to the top of the slate roof.

"Mr. Harcourt. I demand to know immediately who you are."

He hesitated for a moment, then sighed. "Very well. I should have told you long ago, but I feared that it might cast a blight on our relationship."

He doffed his hat in a regal gesture that was intended to look humble. "I am Miles Harcourt, the Marquis of Grantsby, at your service, madam."

"I don't believe you. Truly, Miles, you have no need to make up such a story. The innkeeper might have been daft enough to accept such a fabrication, but I..."

He tilted his head and leaned an elbow against the cushion. "I speak the truth, Juliana. It was my intention to return directly to London after my ship docked, but I had received word just before leaving the Indies that my caretaker and his wife were suddenly called home to Scotland. Since Fordingbridge, where we stayed, is only a little out of the way, I decided to stop by there long enough to attend to properly closing the house until my solicitors can find a trustworthy caretaker."

She put her hand to her mouth. "Then you really are the Marquis of Grantsby?"

"I give you my word. And since we've agreed to be honest, suppose you tell me who you really are?" He ignored her sudden intake of breath. "Don't look so set-down. I want the truth now."

"But I've told you. My name is Juliana Penridge. I am recently widowed."

"Oh, come now. Don't take me for a fool. I know nobility when I meet it. Wouldn't it be less embarrassing to confess now, before I introduce you to my mother?"

Juliana chewed the inside of her cheek. "You're right, of course. I really didn't mean to be secretive, my lord."

He nearly exploded. "My lord...my lord. Isn't this carrying formality a bit far? Surely we can dispense with the title after all we've been through? And why haven't you told me before this?"

Juliana fought to keep her color even. "You must remember that I had no idea what kind of man I had dragged in from the storm. You looked like last year's hedgehog. I kept my true identity a secret purely out of self-preservation."

"I understand. There is no need for an apology."

"It was not intended as an apology," she said tartly. "I am Juliana Penridge, daughter of Johann Vonnegat, fifth son of the Count of Gilsenkirken. My brother, Jules, was born in Germany, but when he was three years old, it became clear my father stood no chance of succession, so he became a British citizen and moved the family to Bath. I was born there." She turned her head to study the line of enormous oak trees that bordered the street. "My father was a scholar of the old school, and we were brought up under the strictest of disciplines. Even so, both Jules and I knew that our parents loved us above all else, and what they did was for our own good. Or so they thought."

"Then all that story about your murdered husband and the stolen fortune was just embroidery to the tapestry you created?"

"Indeed not! Everything I told you was true. My husband was Sir Cedric Penridge, the Right Honorable Earl of Dovington. I merely omitted the fact that I am a woman of title."

"Just a slight oversight."

She lifted a shoulder. "What difference does it make? The title is of little importance now that I have no lands to go with it. Would you have treated me any differently if you had known about my station in life?"

"That, Lady Juliana, is something you will never know."

He put his hand on Nadina's shoulder and gently shook her. "Ah, I believe we have arrived, Mademoiselle Beaurivage. It is time to awaken."

Juliana was aware from the stunned expression on Nadina's face that the young woman had heard every word of the conversation. She regarded Juliana with admiration mixed with a marked degree of curiosity. One look from Juliana silenced the questions for the moment, but Juliana knew it was a temporary respite.

The carriage negotiated the turn through the gate and pulled to a stop in front of the wide entrance, which was flanked on each side by carved marble urns that stood taller than most men. As if by an unheard signal, the oaken doors of the mansion were thrown open and a half-dozen footmen in blue and gold livery scurried to assist Miles and Juliana from the carriage.

The butler, obviously aware of his superior position, stood sedately as he waited to greet them.

"Lord Grantsby, welcome home, sir. 'Tis pleased we are to have you back with us."

"Thank you, Billings. This is Lady Juliana, the Countess of Dovington, who, along with her abigail, Mademoiselle Beaurivage, will be visiting us."

The butler bowed, showing his exquisite training by not betraying the least bit of curiosity. "Welcome to London, my lady. I am at your service," he said, motioning them to precede him into the house.

Juliana, walking alongside Miles, spoke softly, "You don't think for a minute that I intend to stay here, do you?"

"Unless you have a quantity of gold secreted on your person, I hardly think you are in a position to argue."

"I will find work."

"It will take time, Juliana." His eyes crinkled. "Of course, there are always the Wilson sisters, Hariette and Amy. It is conceivable that they might set you up in business as a *Fashionable Impure*, despite the fact that you have become a trifle long in the tooth."

"If you are looking to die soon, my lord, you have chosen the easy path." She would have said more, but a retinue of servants had formed a line inside the great foyer to greet their returning master.

Miles spoke first with his housekeeper, a plump motherly sort with a thick gray-white braid coiled at the nape of her neck. "Mrs. McGrath, you look more beautiful every time I see you."

She basked in his praise, then greeted Juliana with acceptable cordiality mixed with a generous degree of suspicion.

Miles appeared not to notice. He put his hand on her shoulder. "Now, Mrs. McGrath, where can we put Lady Juliana? Is the gold suite ready to receive visitors?"

"Indade, no, me lord. The Lady Louisa has taken it upon herself to move into the gold suite. Mayhap her ladyship would be comfortable in the Oxford suite?"

Juliana noticed his hesitation, then he nodded. "That would be fine. Is my mother at home?"

"The two of them's gone to the linen-draper's on St. James Street."

Miles grinned. "That should keep them most of the afternoon, unless I miss my guess. If you would show Lady Juliana and her abigail to their rooms, I'll ask the footman to see to the luggage."

Mrs. McGrath looked Juliana up and down, no doubt taking note of the widow's black. "This way, my lady. 'Tis up the staircase and down the corridor to the left. Right next to 'is lordship's suite," she added with a sly look that didn't go unnoticed by the waiting footmen. Rather than make a to-do about the unfortunate location of her apartment, Juliana kept silent. She was grateful for the brief reprieve before having to face Miles's mother and the Lady Louisa, whoever she might be.

Upon entering the darkened suite, Mrs. McGrath made her way to the windows and threw back the heavy draperies that had shut out the sunlight.

"This was the lieutenant's apartment afore he was kilt in the war with the Frenchies." She sniffed disdainfully over her shoulder at Nadina. "'Tis clean as can be, though, and will warm up as soon as the maid lights the fire in the grate. Shall I have someone unpack for you?"

Nadina spoke up quickly. "*Non*. I shall unpack for the countess. Would you be good enough to send a cold collation and a pot of tea to our rooms as soon as possible? Afterwards her ladyship will require a hot bath and time to rest."

Mrs. McGrath straightened. "Yes, of course. I'll see to it at once."

As soon as the door closed behind her, Juliana smiled at Nadina. "No one can accuse you of not taking charge."

"*Oui*, madam. It is necessary sometimes. With one such as her you must first get her respect before you can achieve friendship." She folded her hands and looked contrite. "Forgive me. I did not mean to over-step my position."

"Food and a hot bath sounds divine." Juliana looked around the sitting room with its velvet draperies and matching carpet of midnight blue. Two comfortable chairs were placed next to a table by the fireplace, and in an oriel at one side of the room, a desk faced the leaded windows. The bedchamber and dressing room adjoined the sitting room.

"We mustn't get too used to this, Nadina. I plan to find my own lodgings as soon as I can establish myself in a position. You would be well advised to be thinking along the same lines."

Nadina smiled. "With the marquis as your protector, how can you be concerned?"

"My protector! Surely you don't think that he and I...?"

"It is true I have heard you fence words with him, but he is a beautiful man, madam. So strong and so sweet-smelling. Would it be truly so difficult to permit him take care of you in exchange for your favors?"

Juliana felt the red begin to creep up her neck and into her face. "Suffice it to say that I have been taken care of by one man, and he led me from prosperity to the gates of the poorhouse. No thank you, Nadina.

One man was enough. From now on I shall look after myself.''

"How sad. Was your husband a good lover?''

Juliana turned away in an effort to hide her embarrassment. "Apparently there were those who thought he was. As for me, I have no one with whom to compare him.

"Now then, I believe I hear the footman with our luggage.'' She opened the door of a commodious armoire. "As soon as they leave, we must begin to hang up our gowns.'' Juliana was grateful for the interruption, but the look on Nadina's face left little doubt that the girl was not deceived.

CHAPTER SIX

NADINA'S ROOM WAS a small cubicle adjoining the larger suite. After they partook of their simple repast and took turns bathing in the warm water carried in by servants, Nadina saw Juliana safely ensconced in her bed, then retired to her own room.

But Juliana was too excited to sleep. Her thoughts were in a turmoil from the incredible twist of fate. There was still much that she didn't know about Miles Harcourt. How much of what he had originally told her was true, and how much was merely a device to keep her from knowing who he was?

In truth, she could not blame him for his deception. She, too, had been guilty of subterfuge in the unwillingness to risk her few remaining treasures at the hands of an adventurer. With each passing moment she felt the need to know more about him become more pressing. His mother would doubtless clear up some of the mystery.

With mixed emotions Juliana dressed herself in a gown of plain, unadorned black crepe, which Nadina had reluctantly selected from the trunk. A matching cap of crepe de chine covered her hair except for a few stray curls that managed to escape. Before she had a chance to change her mind, Juliana left the room and descended the semicircular flight of stairs to the first floor. A footman, anticipating her indecision, bowed.

"May I direct my lady to the library?"

"Yes, thank you."

They proceeded across the main foyer, which was hung with vibrant tapestries of mythological characters in wooded settings. The footman stopped at a heavily carved door, knocked, then opened it and waited for Juliana to precede him.

"Lady Juliana, the Countess of Dovington," he announced in a clear voice.

Two women were seated at the far end of the room. The elder, a strikingly regal woman with dark brown hair secured by a coronet of braids at the base of her neck, was surely Miles's mother, the marchioness. Neatly crossed ankles were just visible beneath the hem of her deceptively simple pearl-gray gown of watered silk, set off by an exquisitely embroidered fichu in shades of ivory, pink and pale yellow. The ornate rings that adorned two fingers on each hand gave evidence to the fact that the marchioness had no qualms about flaunting her wealth in a ladylike way.

The other woman, who stood as Juliana approached, must be the mysterious Louisa. She was voluptuous in form but not indecently so. Juliana admitted grudgingly that most men would consider her quite a beauty, in a full-blown way. She, too, was every inch the lady of quality, but a second glance gave Juliana the distinct impression that there was a basic restlessness in her that the woman took great pains to conceal.

Her hands clasped lightly in front of her, Juliana swept across the room toward them. Approaching the marchioness, she dropped a practiced curtsy.

"Lady Grantsby, I hope I am not intruding."

"Not at all, madam. Louisa and I were just speaking of you."

Juliana smothered her sigh of relief. "Then his lordship has apprised you of my presence. I regret that our arrival was so unannounced, but..."

The younger woman interrupted. "Not entirely. We have been expecting Miles for more than a week now, and the delay caused us no little concern, I assure you." She plucked at the tatted bodice of her violet gown, drawing attention to her full bosom. Dark hair spilled in a cluster of ringlets from the bottom edge of a violet lace cap. Juliana noted with amusement that Louisa's eyes were also a delicate shade of violet fringed with thick, dark lashes. The effect was strikingly feminine.

It was clear from the expression on the woman's face that she held Juliana to blame for Miles's tardiness. The marchioness waved her hand in annoyance.

"Louisa, dear. Don't trouble our guest with needless recrimination. Lady Juliana Penridge, may I present Lady Louisa Danforth Harcourt, my daughter-in-law."

Lady Louisa's bosom lifted as she stood up straight and inclined her head in reluctant acknowledgment. Juliana reached for the back of a wing chair on which to support herself. Miles, the swine, had lied to her. He was, after all, married. It took all of her self-control to drop a sedate curtsy and say all the appropriate things.

Fortunately, the footman chose that moment to announce Miles. The bath and change of clothing had worked wonders on his appearance. No longer the rough seaman in twill and coarse fustian, he stood tall and immaculate in fawn breeches and a matching waistcoat topped off with a perfectly folded tall white starcher; the very picture of a gentleman of the haute monde.

He first bent to place a kiss on his mother's cheek, then turned to include them all in his breezy smile. "Forgive me, Juliana. I assumed you would still be resting. I had intended to be here to make the introductions."

The marchioness waggled her hand. "It has been taken care of, Miles. Sit down, everyone. Do be seated. I can't abide everyone towering over me."

Juliana was suddenly conscious of her own height. She was tall for a woman, but it had never bothered her until now. Louisa was a good head shorter than she. And what tiny feet! Juliana tucked her own feet carefully under the folds of her gown as Miles seated her in the wing chair across from the marchioness.

"Now then," the marchioness demanded, emphasizing her words with the thump of her gold-handled walking cane. "What's this about you saving my son's life?"

"Well, I, I think that's putting it a bit strongly, Lady Grantsby. I merely discovered him lying in a ditch along the verge during a rainstorm and put him to bed."

The marchioness' eyebrows shot up a good inch. "Indeed! You did this without assistance from anyone else?"

"I had no choice, madam. We were quite alone at the country house."

The marchioness turned from her waist to pierce Miles with her hawk's gaze, while at the same time directing her remark to Juliana. "But I understood that your abigail arrived with you."

Too late, Juliana saw the frustration on Miles's face. No doubt he had led his mother to believe that Nadina had been with them throughout the entire country house episode.

The devil take him, Juliana thought. *I'll not lie to protect his skin.*

Juliana folded her hands to keep them from shaking. "Forgive me, madam, but you have perhaps misunderstood. It was only last night that I met Mademoiselle Beaurivage, who is serving as my lady's maid. I happened on the country house quite by accident when I was evicted from a public coach on the way to London. Mr. Harcourt, I—I mean Lord Grantsby and I were both forced to take shelter in an unoccupied country estate."

The marchioness nearly blustered in her disbelief. "Surely you were aware that the estate at Fordingbridge is King's Grant, our country home?"

Juliana shot a quick look at Miles, who raised his eyes to the ceiling. She shook her head. "There were many things I did not know then, your ladyship. It was a very trying period in my life." She looked defiantly at Miles, who leveled his gaze at her, daring her to admit how much she enjoyed their isolation.

His voice was dry. "I assure you, Mother, that we were most careful to observe the social graces. Juliana saw to that."

Louisa, her eyes as round as the gold snuffbox that lay on the table beside her, leaned forward. "Dear heaven, what are we going to do, Mother Harcourt? If news of this indiscretion gets out, we shall all be ruined." She fanned her hand quickly in front of her face. "Lady Jersey would give her year's allowance to get her teeth into a morsel like this." She looked horrified. "At the very least, they will take back our bid to Almack's."

Miles's moustache lifted in amusement. "Don't be so dramatic, Louisa. No one will ever know unless you tell them."

The marchioness thumped her cane on the floor. "She's right, you know. It's bound to get out. The servants will have it spread over London as surely as if it appeared in the *Morning Post*."

Juliana stood. "I truly regret this more than I can say. The best thing for me to do would be to leave tonight and take Nadina with me."

Louisa went white around the mouth. "Don't be a fool. That would only serve to make things worse. Polite Society would accuse us of casting you into the street. Miles, darling. You must think of something. You are so clever." She grasped the arms of the straightbacked chair in her hands and leaned forward. "I know. We could say that she is your long-lost aunt."

Juliana felt her face go red as she bit back a heated reply. Miles looked contemptuous.

"Be sensible, Louisa. Juliana is far too young to be my aunt." He grinned. "Of course we could say that she and I were married the night I returned from my voyage."

As in one voice, the women chorused "No!"

The marchioness placed both hands atop the crook of her cane and leaned over it. "At least we agree on one thing. No, there is no other way. We must stand firm and face the scandalmongers down."

Miles nodded his approval. "I think you're right, Mother. No one would dare challenge our word."

Juliana was distraught. "I'm dreadfully sorry about all this. I shall leave in two days at the very latest."

The marchioness straightened. "Unfortunately, I cannot permit that. You must continue to remain under my protection until the gossip has dissipated. Otherwise we shall be made to look the fool. Do you agree to abide by my wishes?"

Juliana felt as if a trap were closing around her. "I suppose I must, if that is the only solution."

"Very well, then. It's settled. We'll say no more about it. You are simply a guest in this house, no more, no less."

Miles grinned hugely at Juliana from behind his mother's chair. As for Louisa, Juliana was hard put to tell whether the sparks her eyes sent out were from anger or a threat of vengeance. Either way, it boded troubled times ahead.

Somehow Juliana managed to get through the next two days. The state of her wardrobe required almost constant attention. Several times a day she thanked a kindly providence for having sent Nadina to her. Nadina, with her quiet ways and her eagerness to help, soon made friends among the servants. Martha McGinty, abigail to Lady Louisa, became a particularly close confidante, much to Juliana's surprise. While Nadina was young, slender and attractive, Martha was nearing thirty, dumpy, with pendulous breasts and hips that were ill-concealed beneath her dun-colored full-skirted uniform.

Although Martha was closemouthed around Juliana, she was always polite and respectful. If Lady Louisa had attempted to poison Martha's mind against Juliana, Martha gave no indication.

It was through Martha that Nadina was kept apprised of the household gossip. It was also through Martha that Nadina was able to discover the relationship between Miles and Louisa. Nadina lost no time in confiding the information to Juliana.

They were mending the lace on a cap and fichu when the truth came out. Juliana stared at Nadina. "You mean to tell me that Miles is not actually married to Louisa?"

"*Oui.* She is his sister-in-law. Lord Grantsby's brother, a certain Sir Archibald Harcourt, the baronet, was an officer who was killed in battle over a year ago."

Juliana slowly let out her breath. "It appears I have done Miles a disservice. He was telling the truth, after all."

"So it would seem, madam." They looked at each other and smiled with shared pleasure. "Isn't it *splendide* to find a man one can trust?"

"Trust? I wouldn't care to go that far, Nadina. Miles does have a way of twisting things at his convenience."

"*Oui.* He is human, no? But what a beautiful man he is. One could learn to accept a little inconvenience for a man such as he. I think madam agrees with me. I can see it in her face when she looks at him."

Juliana blushed. "And you are an incurable romantic, Nadina. Tell me," she said, in an effort to change the subject, "have you no young man to whom you'd give your heart?"

Nadina's face pinched together at the thought. "There was such a one a few years ago, but he is dead now."

"You must have been a mere child."

"Not so young as not to know a woman's desire. I think perhaps he was the only man I shall ever love."

"I can't believe that. Someday you'll find a man you want to marry."

Nadina looked shocked. "But of course. I will marry within three years, I think."

"Then you have someone in mind."

"Not precisely, madam. But I must find someone before I become old and too ugly to attract a man of means." She looked up to see the startled expression on Juliana's face.

"Do not be surprised. One does not have to wait for the grand passion to take a husband. *Pour l'amour de Dieu!* If that were true, I fear few women would ever marry." She put the thread between her teeth and snapped it with a quick jerk. "Men have it all, you know: the right to choose, the right to possess. The least we can do is make them pay well for it. Is that not so?"

Juliana shook her head. "I don't know, Nadina. In truth, my husband was a cad. In all honesty, I cannot grieve over his passing, and yet something inside me believes that marriage to the right man could bring joy beyond belief."

"If that is true, madam, and I pray God it is, shouldn't you be doing something about it?"

"I beg your pardon?"

"Forgive me. I do not mean to offend, but your gowns, madam. They are very ugly. And your hair! It suffers from lack of skilled hand to dress it. It would seem to me that you have worn the black long enough for a husband who deserved his own inglorious fate."

"But what would people think? It has been only a matter of months since Cedric was killed."

Nadina threw up her hands. *"Pour l'amour de Dieu!* At least they will be talking about you, madam. Is not that far better than going unnoticed?"

Juliana laughed. "It's an interesting idea, though I'm not sure the marchioness would agree with it." Before she could change her mind, she jumped up. "Nevertheless, I think I shall surprise them all at dinner this evening. Come. Help me choose something scandalous to wear."

It sounded so easy when they simply talked about it, but actually going through with it was another affair. Catching a glimpse of her image in the tall ormolu mirror at the top of the stairs, Juliana had second thoughts. Nadina had swept her hair up into a golden coronet spiked with a cascade of tiny saffron-colored silk roses on the left side. The topaz silk gown with its high neckline and full skirt could hardly be called scandalous, but it made Juliana look years younger.

To give Cedric his due, he had known how to select her gowns to make the most of her face and figure. The last time she had worn the topaz silk was the night she had found him in a compromising situation with the Viscountess Elderbrook. Juliana had sworn she would never wear the gown again, but beggars could not be choosers.

Still, she wondered what reaction she would receive from the family. Miles would not be likely to criticize her, she thought, remembering the night at the country house when they had danced to the tune from the music box. Of course, things were different here, and Miles was a different man. He went to great pains to keep the peace and stay in his mother's good graces. When Miles had suggested that he take Juliana for a ride in Hyde Park without benefit of chaperon, the marchioness had become livid.

She had waved her cane in the air, as if to strike him. "There will be none of that, my boy, while I'm alive. Enough mischief has already been done. We'll not compound it. If you wish to take her ladyship for a drive, then see to it that she is properly chaperoned."

Miles had protested weakly, "What need is there of a chaperon? The countess is a widow, mother. She is long past the age . . ."

Juliana hadn't cared to hear any more. The question of her age had arisen more than once, admittedly in jest, but she had begun to feel as though she were in her dotage.

Miles had given in to his mother's demands, and they had taken Nadina and Louisa along in the carriage. Somehow, though, all the pleasure had gone out of the day.

Tonight, seeing herself in splendid dress, gave Juliana a feeling of power that was entirely unexpected. She descended toward the waiting footman, pleasantly aware of the look of admiration he failed to conceal.

They were waiting, the three of them, with glasses of sherry in hand, at one end of the salon where it was their habit to meet before dinner was served. Juliana thought of it as the throne room, for it was here, in a glassed-in alcove, that the marchioness sat each morning with her family and servants gathered around her to receive instructions for the day.

They looked up as she entered, and the gasp was audible down the length of the room. It caused Juliana to hesitate in midstep.

"Come here, madam!" the marchioness ordered, punctuating her words with a resounding thump of her cane.

Juliana lifted her chin, walked swiftly down the polished floor and negotiated a graceful curtsy. "My lady?"

"So this is how you were brought up to show your respect to the dear departed. Go to your room at once, madam, and don't come downstairs until you are properly clothed in widow's black.''

Juliana's heart pounded in her chest in the same way it had at Miss Haverstock's Academy for Young Ladies, when she had been wrongly accused of pinching food from the kitchen safe. She wasn't guilty then, and she didn't feel guilty now. But this time she would stand up for herself.

Juliana folded her hands primly at her waist. ''Forgive me, Lady Grantsby. I can no longer bring myself to mourn a man whom I could not respect, let alone love. Cedric was a cruel and brutal man. I am not sorry he is dead. To continue to wear widow's black would be deceitful.''

Louisa burst out. ''But . . . but what will people think?''

Miles raised his gaze to the ceiling. ''My God. Who cares what people think?''

The marchioness thumped her cane. ''We must live in Polite Society, Miles, and conform to its dictates.''

Juliana's voice was so soft that when she spoke it seemed as if they each held their breath.

''Ah, but my lady. We must first live with ourselves and our own conscience.''

Miles applauded. ''Well put, Juliana.''

Louisa looked beseechingly at the marchioness. ''Mother Harcourt, don't listen to them. We've so much to lose if we should get the snub from the ladies at Almack's.''

The marchioness nodded. ''Yes. You must do as I say, Countess. In the privacy of our home you may dress appropriately, but in public you must follow convention. In a few weeks, perhaps..."

None of them had noticed Miles leave the room, but when the marchioness turned to face him, he was not there. The butler brought a tray to Juliana with a glass of sherry. She had scarcely touched it when Miles returned.

He faced them, hands on hips, a defiant expression in his eyes. "I have just ordered that the gowns in question be burned. Now, we'll hear no more talk of widow's weeds. I've always maintained they are an affront to one's sensibilities."

The marchioness appeared completely flabbergasted. "Miles, I've never known you to be so high-handed." Her voice rang with sarcasm. "It would appear to me that you have been too long at sea."

Juliana and Miles were aware at the same instant, that his mother echoed Juliana's own words back at the country house. A secret look passed between them, and they both struggled to hide their mirth.

There was no amusement on Louisa's face. Only a grim set to her mouth that betrayed a reluctant determination to remain silent. Juliana suspected it was only a temporary reprieve.

Dinner was subdued, thanks to the earlier confrontation, but as usual, the food was delicious. It began with a thin turtle soup, then continued through the fish and meat courses and ended with an airy, rich almond fluff and platters of assorted fruit. When they were finished, they adjourned to the drawing room where Louisa favored them with some classical renditions on the pianoforte.

Miles maneuvered Juliana into a chair some distance from his mother, and they were able to talk quietly without being overheard.

"Juliana, you look decidedly provocative tonight."

"Despite my advanced years?" Juliana asked tartly.

"Don't be so prickly. It will be many years before you become too long in the tooth to be considered beautiful." He pursed his mouth. "Or were you just looking for a compliment?"

"I was not." She leaned closer to him. "I owe you a debt of gratitude for standing up to your mother tonight."

"My pleasure. Black depresses me. But it was you who surprised me. Not many women would have the courage to disagree with a direct order from her ladyship."

At that moment the butler entered the room to deliver a note on a silver salver. The marchioness opened it, then threw it on the floor in disgust. She thumped her cane on the floor, and Louisa stopped playing as abruptly as if she had been struck.

"Wh-what is it? Have I displeased you, your ladyship?"

"Oh, stop blithering and come here, all of you."

When they had seated themselves closer to her, the marchioness motioned to the note on the floor. "It's as I feared. The gossipmongers have got wind of the fact that Miles has brought a woman home with him. Lady Heathecote has begged my leave to give a reception in honor of Miles and Lady Juliana."

Louisa rapidly fanned herself as if to keep from fainting. "How dreadful! What are we going to do?"

"Do? Why, we must give our own party, of course, before she has the opportunity to preempt us."

The marchioness leaned back against the winged chair. "Not a ball or a rout. That would make it seem too important. We might give a soiree; dinner with dancing afterward, or even a musical evening. Just a few guests. But it must be within the week. The invitations must be sent tomorrow."

It was obvious from the start that the marchioness wasn't asking for advice, but Juliana felt compelled to speak. "I wonder, Lady Grantsby, about the advisability of linking Miles's and my name together in such a way? Would it not be more prudent to give the party in honor of the Marquis' return from America?"

The marchioness looked surprised. "Indeed. You make a good point. Of course, at the same time you must be introduced as a guest of honor, or the gossip would not be put down." She nodded as if agreeing with herself.

"Oh, drat! I've clean forgot. My secretary has gone to Brighton to be with her ailing mother. Now what shall we do about invitations?"

Juliana spoke up. "If you merely need someone to write the invitations, I will be happy to do so."

Miles grinned widely. "An excellent suggestion, Mother. Juliana writes a splendid hand. I happened to see a note she wrote back at the country house." Juliana's look was calculated to wither the ruffle on his starched high neckcloth.

They talked for a while about whom to invite, what dancing troupe was in town, what opera singer might be available. The marchioness was enjoying the unexpected diversion, and Louisa, for some reason, seemed to soften her prickly attitude towards Juliana.

Miles was clearly bored. "If you ladies will excuse me, I will leave the planning to you and take myself to the library to look over the shipping company's books."

Louisa's mouth drooped. "Darling, we see so little of you."

"My dear sister-in-law, I remember these party planning to-dos. You won't even know I've left the room."

Later, after the marchioness had said her good nights, Juliana was left alone with Louisa, who immediately turned to her.

"It was very decent of you, Lady Juliana, to suggest that Miles's name be the only one on the invitation. I must confess, I did suspect that you were some kind of adventuress out to steal Miles away from me."

"Indeed?" Juliana was too confused and surprised to speak.

"Quite so. Of course, we haven't made the announcement yet, but everyone knows that Miles and I plan to marry in a year or so. It's the custom in this family, you know. If a brother dies, the next unmarried brother in line becomes the protector of the widow. Alas, since I lost my dear Archibald to the French, I am left alone and helpless." She fluttered her violet fan rapidly in front of her face, then snapped it shut and touched the tip to her cheek in a winsome gesture. Her laughter floated like dust motes in the lamplight.

"Of course, I am far from destitute. I stand to inherit my family's shipping business when my father dies. Between us, Miles and I will control the second largest shipping company in the world." She laughed again and pulled a dark ringlet across her chin. "It is an enormous relief to know that I have Miles to turn to, but it is even better to know that I have something to give in return."

Juliana's thoughts were in a state of turmoil. She made all the appropriate responses, then hastened to excuse herself. All she wanted was to be alone.

There it was. The truth of her own situation. Lady Louisa had made it all too clear that Miles belonged to her. She had everything to offer him; youth, beauty, money, position, and yes, even tradition. Whatever illusions Juliana held that something might come of her friendship with Miles were pure fantasy. But dear heaven, how it hurt. It hurt beyond belief.

CHAPTER SEVEN

LADY GRANTSBY'S IDEA of a small gathering bore no single resemblance to what Juliana had in mind when she offered to handwrite the invitations. Fifteen guests grew to twenty, and in no time the number had jumped to forty-five.

"How many people do you think will accept, your ladyship?" Juliana asked, happy to rest her hand for a while.

"Why, all of them, if they have any sense." A bemused expression flitted across Lady Grantsby's face as she paused on the needlepoint she was stitching for a wedding gift for the Princess Charlotte. "Of course, I would excuse a woman if she were in the midst of childbirth, or a man if he were on his deathbed."

Juliana started to laugh, but realized in time that the marchioness was not jesting. She doubtless enjoyed more than her share of power in the haute monde. Nadina had learned from backstairs gossip that the marchioness, when she was a young woman, had been a chamber lady to the queen. Of course, Drecinda Harcourt's influence could no longer compete with the Committee of Seven who controlled the vouchers to the subscription balls at Almack's, but the marchioness was close to Lady Jersey and Countess Lieven.

That fact alone was enough to guarantee her a special place in Polite Society.

As expected, the responses began to arrive just a few short hours after the messengers delivered the envelopes. No one sent regrets.

It was left to Louisa to arrange the entertainment, with Lady Grantsby's supervision, of course. An invitation had gone out to Madame Caranari, who had agreed to sing several selections from *Semiramide* and other operas.

Miles used business pressures to escape the fuss and bother of a household under siege. He confided to Juliana that once his appointments were out of the way he often spent the late afternoons at a gathering with John Murray and his friends at the publisher's drawing room on Albermarle Street.

"Indeed?" Juliana exclaimed. "I had no idea you were inclined toward a tête-à-tête with such noted scholars."

Miles grinned. "It pleases me to keep you guessing. You so easily become indignant."

"And you, sir, are an unconscionable tease."

"Is that in addition to being the wastrel you attributed to me when we were living together at the country house?"

"Miles Harcourt! You are insufferable. In no way could one describe that brief encounter as our having lived together. We merely by chance shared the same domicile."

He took her elbow and led her to a large gilt mirror. "Look for yourself, Juliana. I was right. Indignation becomes you."

Juliana had no choice but to study her reflection. It was true. The heightened color in her face was becoming. It had been years since she looked so alive, so vital. She was reminded of the country house and the night they had dressed for dinner.

If her reflection pleased her, the image of the two of them standing so close together was uncommonly disturbing. Anyone would have said they made an attractive couple, and for one brief moment she toyed with the idea. Juliana Harcourt. It had a pleasant sound.

"What are you thinking, Juliana? You seem to have left me."

She was suddenly aware of the warmth of his hand still cupping her elbow; aware of his breath that stirred the fine hair at the back of her neck. She pulled quickly away and walked toward the hallway. At the last moment she turned back to face him.

"If you must know, I was thinking about your fiancée. Louisa would have misunderstood if she had chanced to come upon us just then."

"No. Wait, Juliana."

Before he could continue, Juliana whirled around and sped up the staircase to her room.

Nadina nearly dropped the gown she was holding when Juliana flung open the door. "*Mon Dieu!* You startled me, madam. Is something amiss?"

"Nothing out of the ordinary."

Nadina laughed. "*Oui.* Then it must be Lord Grantsby. No? Whenever I see that look in your eyes, I know that you have been with him again."

"Don't be absurd. The man is impossible. He makes me so angry. I hate him. I do truly hate him."

Nadina smiled. "*Oui*, madam. I can see that."

"Wipe that missish look off your face and stop being so muzzy-headed."

"*Oui*, madam."

Juliana sighed. "Forgive me, Nadina. I shouldn't speak to you that way. You are my one true friend."

"And you mine, madam. It hurts me to see you so unsettled. Can you not admit to yourself that you are attracted to Lord Grantsby and would like nothing better than for him to offer for you?"

"You are most certainly mistaken, Nadina. The man is too cocksure of himself, too full of pride to commit himself to wedlock. He is the kind of man who would dance a jig with a woman, then leave her when he tired of the tune." She smoothed her hand over the panniers at each side of her gown. "Besides, I have only recently learned that he and Louisa are pledged to each other."

Nadina looked shocked. "Betrothed?"

"Not officially. Louisa is the widow of Miles's brother. It is customary in the Harcourt family for the unmarried surviving brother to take on the responsibilities of the deceased. It is just a question of time until they will announce their betrothal."

"His lordship told you this?"

"Good lackaday! We have not talked of such things."

"*Oui*, then it must have been the Lady Louisa?"

"Suffice it to say that I have learned better than to entertain thoughts of marriage to the marquis."

"Those two are not suited to each other. This news is very sad to hear."

"The truth often is, Nadina. At any rate, this conversation leaves much to be desired." She picked up a gown of pale blue silk and held it to her chin. "Whatever am I going to wear to the party the marchioness is giving next week?"

Nadina's eyes sparkled. "Something divinely wicked?"

Juliana laughed. "Just the opposite, I think. Something demure and nunnish. We wouldn't want the gossips to think that I was compromised while Miles and I were staying at the country house. And after all, I'm just coming out of mourning."

"*Oui*, but at the same time you must look *ravissant*. All of London society will be watching you."

"Um, perhaps that gold brocade with the green velvet panniers." Juliana saw the expression on Nadina's face. "What is it? You don't think it would be appropriate?"

Nadina shrugged. "It would be adequate, madam, but the fullness of skirt is somewhat passé." She picked up a simple ivory linen. "Now this would follow the trend toward the Grecian mode, but it needs something." She pulled open the drawer of a chest redolent of cedar chips. "*Oui*. Now if we add this silk shawl and drape it on an angle," she said as she placed it on Juliana's shoulder. "Voilá! It is *charmant*, is it not? And the shell pink is perfect with your complexion."

"If only I had not sold my sapphire necklace. It would have been just what I need."

"*Que non!* Then they would have seen nothing but jewels. This way they will first notice you."

Juliana laughed. "How is it that you know so much about fashion?"

Nadina looked surprised. "Why, I am French, madam."

Apparently that explained it. They settled on a pair of ivory satin slippers to complete the ensemble. Nadina vowed to create a hairstyle that would complement the gown and catch every eye in the grand salon where the festivities were to take place.

When Juliana ventured a look at the assembly room early in the afternoon on the day of the party, she was astounded. It could easily have held a hundred people without their having to rub elbows. The walls were draped in gold silk, held in place by ostrich plumes. Midnight blue velvet chairs provided ample seating yet allowed enough room for people to circulate. At one side, French doors gave way to a view of the formal garden, complete with fountains, shadowed walks and a rose garden.

Everything had happened so quickly that Juliana was hard put to believe it was not just a fantasy, but when the marchioness called her to the salon to receive her instructions, Juliana came swiftly back to earth.

"Remember, my dear, that the sole reason for your being included in the festivities is to put to rest the gossip surrounding your unfortunate stay at the country house."

Juliana started to say something, but the marchioness silenced her with a gesture. "Suffice it to say that

Miles will be the center of interest. You will remain in the background once you have left the receiving line. Do you understand?''

"Quite." Juliana's voice was cold. "I have no desire to display myself. Were it my decision, I would choose to be a hundred miles from here."

The marchioness peered at her over the top of her spectacles. "Indeed?"

"Most certainly. I look forward to the day when I can find employment and move into my own quarters."

"How odd. You do not impress me as one of the working class. I vaguely remember your parents. We met many years ago at a gala at some remote Cornwall estate. Heatherfield, I believe. Belonging to the Duke and Duchess of Heatherwood."

"It's possible, though I couldn't say for certain. My parents were not socially inclined but preferred to keep to themselves."

"I doubt that they would approve your hiring yourself out as a governess or going into commerce."

Juliana sighed. "Were it not for the unfortunate marriage my father arranged for me, I would not have to seek employment. I hold no grudges, however. Truthfully, I rather look forward to the prospect of acting on my own."

"Hmph. Face up to it, madam. You have no dowry. Your prospects are limited, to say the least. Take my advice and find a husband while you still have the looks to snare one."

Juliana gripped the arms of the chair to keep from losing her temper. "Thank you, your ladyship. I shall consider your advice. In the meantime I shall be looking for employment as well as a place to live.''

"Kindly refrain from speaking of it at the party tonight.''

Juliana was fast becoming furious. ''Forgive me, your ladyship, but I do not require lessons in deportment.''

The marchioness was properly if quietly set down. ''Be that as it may, I can only hope that you will remember your upbringing.'' Seeing the set look on Juliana's face, she tempered her remarks. ''I can't fault you, my dear, for hoping to gain some control over your life. And I must say that you were most helpful in writing the invitations. Your handwriting is the finest I've seen of late.''

Juliana slowly let our her breath. ''Thank you. I'm pleased to help in any way that I can.''

The marchioness nodded, then thumped the floor. ''Enough. It is time that we retired to our rooms to dress for the party. Be ready to come downstairs when I send the maid to your suite.''

Juliana didn't stop to linger. She had scored at least a few points with the lady dragon, and she wasn't inclined to risk losing ground. It occurred to Juliana that her ladyship respected her for having taken a stand and holding fast to it. Needless to say, it felt good to refuse to be pushed around. Cedric had taught her long ago how miserable life could be under the thumb of an arrogant tyrant.

THE SUMMONS CAME to make her appearance downstairs at nearly the same instant that Nadina put the finishing touches to Juliana's coiffure. She was grateful for the fuss and bother that kept her from thinking about how to get through the approaching festivities. Nadina refused to let her go until she had taken one last look.

"*Oui.* You will do, madam. You will be the envy of everyone, I think."

Juliana knew she was teasing, but in truth she was pleased with her reflection in the mirror. Nadina had been right about the dress. Instead of following the fashion of gathers just below the bodice of the ivory linen gown, Nadine had crisscrossed a length of gold rope into a girdle that snugged the dress in at the waistline, as well as below the bust. The softly feminine curves were accentuated to an inviting degree, but when Juliana drifted the silk shawl across one shoulder, it partially concealed her shape. The effect served to invite a closer look.

At the doorway, the little Irish maid was becoming anxious. "Countess, please, we must hurry. The marchioness will be sending the footman to fetch us."

Nadina nodded. "Go along, madam. You will be the sensation of the evening."

IN SOME RESPECTS Nadina's prediction came true, but it was not the way Juliana had hoped. From the moment when she entered the room, all eyes turned toward her. Juliana saw little friendship reflected in them. Apparently the scandalmongers had done their work. Although no woman was so obvious as to draw away, neither did anyone go out of her way to venture a pleasant word.

Juliana hoped that Miles might rescue her, but he had little opportunity, so surrounded was he by dowagers hoping to present their unspoken-for daughters.

It was small comfort that Louisa fared little better. The women, mostly close acquaintances of the marchioness, were well aware that family tradition dictated, or at least suggested, that Louisa be the natural choice as the next marchioness of Grantsby. Those matrons who had eligible daughters were determined to thwart tradition.

Juliana was startled out of her reveries when a rosy-cheeked young lieutenant bowed low in front of her. She remembered that his name was Roger Beekman. He ran nervous fingers through a thatch of unruly blond hair. "May I beg the honor of the first dance, my lady?"

Juliana was about to ask him if he knew what he was doing, but the music touched her spirit of adventure.

"The honor is mine, Lieutenant."

He led her to their place in line, and they waited for the reel to begin. Juliana looked up at him. He was very young, and with a twinge of pain she realized how much the freckled-faced boy resembled her brother. Jules, too, had once stood tall and proud in his uniform.

"Lieutenant, you must know you are risking your reputation by dancing with me."

"Indeed, Countess. I would risk even my life for a few moments of your attention."

Juliana's eyes opened wide. "I beg your pardon?"

He had the grace to blush. "I... There have been stories about your—about how you—"

Her voice was dry. "There is no need to continue, Lieutenant. I would beg you to remember that I have only recently come out of mourning for my husband, the late Earl of Dovington. The stories you may have heard are a complete fabrication."

His face fell. "Oh. I'm sorry. I mean I'm sorry for the stories, not sorry the stories are not true."

Juliana was unable to conceal a smile. "Be honest, young man. Wouldn't you prefer it the other way around? What else prompted you to ask me for a dance but the remote chance that you might indulge in a bit of dalliance?"

"Your ladyship!" His neck turned red all the way up to his ears.

Before he could protest further, they were caught up in the movement of the other dancers. When he returned to her side, his face had taken on a pasty-white look.

"I beg of you, Lady Juliana, please do not think too badly of me. I was told that you might be an easy..."

She touched her fingers to his mouth. "Hush. Someone has played fast and easy with you. You must learn, Lieutenant, not to take life so seriously."

"If I could make amends?"

Juliana shook her head, then changed her mind. "You could tell me who told you this disgusting tale."

He was torn by indecision but finally capitulated. "It was Sir Alexi Rustegian. The man in the green velvet waistcoat."

"Thank you, Lieutenant. I'm ever grateful to you."

"Grateful enough to have another dance, Countess?"

"My, you are getting brave. Forgive me, Lieutenant, but it would be unseemly for us to dance another reel so soon. Perhaps later."

After that, the mood of the party seemed to change. The lieutenant had broken the ice, and several men approached to ask Juliana to dance. For the first time she was grateful that Cedric had hired a dance master to teach her the art of ballroom dancing. She was graceful and light on her feet, and it made her feel young and beautiful to be the center of attention.

They had just finished a sprightly march when the bottle-green waistcoat approached her. Sir Alexi bowed deeply, pointing a toe in an affected way. "My lady. Sir Alexi Malancoff Rustegian, at your service. May I beg the honor of this dance? I understand it is to be a waltz."

Juliana smiled sweetly and said in a voice that carried some distance across the room, "Thank you, Sir Alexi. I wouldn't dance with you if you were the last man on earth."

He looked completely flabbergasted. "But your ladyship, what have I done to deserve such an insult? You owe me an apology."

"Sir. If I were a man, I would call you out. Suffice it to say that you are such a superb storyteller that you will surely be able to think of something titillating to explain my behavior."

His face was livid as he wheeled around and stalked from the room. As Juliana planned, the scene had not gone unnoticed. There was a dead silence. Then from somewhere in the back of the room, a woman tittered. And then another and another. Juliana stayed frozen in place. Then suddenly, Miles approached her. She saw him as if in a dream—his blue eyes fringed with thick, dark lashes, drawing her to a place of infinite peace and safety.

"You seem to be in want of a glass of punch, my lady. May I fetch it for you?"

She was unable to speak.

He took her arm. "Or would you care to dance? I think they are about to play a waltz."

She nodded. "So I'm told. I've come to enjoy the waltz."

He led her onto the floor, and the music began. At first they were the only couple caught up in the music, but seconds later the silence broke into a crackle and gabble that sounded like a farmyard. Then other couples moved onto the floor.

Miles held her at arm's length as they whirled around the room. "You seem to have had your share of partners tonight. I thought I'd never get the chance to dance with you."

"You jest, Miles. I saw the way the women flocked around you. And you were enjoying every second of it. I couldn't have been farther from your thoughts."

"You are wrong, Juliana. From the moment the music began, I thought of no one and nothing but the night we danced to the tune of the music box at my country house."

A quick vision of the two of them, caught up in the spell of their isolation, flashed before her mind, and she trembled.

He pulled her closer to him. "You were beautiful then, but tonight your beauty defies description."

Juliana leaned away and leveled her gaze at him. "No doubt you were right in your assessment. I was sadly in need of a lady's maid."

He pulled her close again, so close that she could feel the pounding of his heart. "Can you not take a jest?"

"I can, but can Louisa? She was watching us until a moment ago. Now I fear she has slipped out the door. You should go after her, Miles."

"Now? She is perfectly safe. I am not accountable for her vagaries."

"Doesn't it bother you that her feelings might be hurt?"

"Of course, but it is none of my doing." He whirled her around abruptly, causing her to miss a step.

"I'm sorry," she said. "My mind was on Louisa."

"If you're going to apologize, you would be well advised to save it for the Russian diplomat. It was his nephew whom you insulted so blatantly."

"He deserved it. The man has been spreading vicious rumors about us."

"You must learn to ignore rumors. If I'd slept with all the women credited to me, I'd have to be over a hundred."

Juliana looked up at him. "Your modesty is overwhelming and quite unexpected, considering your previous boastings."

Miles executed a few experimental turns, then settled into a steady pattern. Juliana prodded him. "You've nothing to say to that?"

"Nothing." His grin dug like a gnat into the surface of her composure.

She fixed him with her gaze. "Just how many women have you...?"

"Come, Juliana. Do you really want to know?"

She thought it over for the briefest of moments. "No, I don't. Truly, Miles, I'm sorry I asked."

"Why change now? Really, Juliana. You are not like other women. I feel a freedom with you that I have yet to experience with another woman."

"Freedom? Does that mean a license to do and say whatever you please?"

He smiled. "Not precisely. Have I not respected you as a woman?"

"You have caused me no end of embarrassment. You have teased me, you have harassed me, you have..."

"But I've respected you, no?" She didn't answer, and they danced for a while without speaking.

When the music stopped, he slowly released her and bowed deeply. She dropped a curtsy and waited for him to escort her back to her chair. Instead he took her lace-gloved hands in his.

"The answer to your question is, not enough."

Juliana's eyes widened. "I beg your pardon, sir!"

He didn't look the least bit affronted. "I'll not be content until I have also known you, Juliana."

Her mouth became suddenly dry. "Stop it, Miles. We shouldn't be talking this way. It's improper. We aren't alone at your country house now."

"More's the pity."

Juliana couldn't argue that point. Neither did she have the opportunity, for the marchioness was descending upon them, her gold-headed cane brandished in front of her like a deadly weapon.

CHAPTER EIGHT

To THOSE WHO FAILED to look sharply, the marchioness was in an amiable mood, but Juliana had come to recognize that kindled fire in her eyes. The marchioness took Miles's arm. "My dear, Lady Jersey is asking for you. It would be prudent to request the next dance."

He bowed. "As you wish, Mother." He looked uncertainly at Juliana, but the marchioness intercepted the passage of arms.

"Do not concern yourself, Miles. I would have a word with the countess."

Juliana mentally drew her lines of defence. "Yes, your ladyship?"

The marchioness nodded to a door at the end of the room. "We can be alone there. Come." She stomped off, punctuating each step with a thrust of her cane.

Once the door closed behind them, the marchioness confronted her. "Do you have any idea what mischief you have done tonight, madam?"

"I . . . I'm afraid not, Lady Grantsby."

"You've probably caused an international incident, that's all. The man you chose to insult in front of everyone was the nephew of the wife of the Russian ambassador. I'll warrant you've not heard the last of that, my girl.''

Juliana's knees weakened, but she managed to remain standing. "I'm sorry. I had no idea. The man is a Cyprian at heart. He is also guilty of spreading falsehoods about Miles and me.''

"Indeed. Suffice it to say that he will have a good story to tell now. And its foundation in truth will only add credence to the other tales.''

"I was wrong, and I admit that, Lady Grantsby. I confess that I simply yielded to an uncontrollable impulse.''

The marchioness seemed to chew it over in her mind. "I would ask you to make a public apology, but the man has seen fit to take his leave.''

"Just as well,'' Juliana murmured. "I could not in good conscience offer an honest apology.''

"Indeed? Indeed!'' The marchioness pounded her cane against the floor. "Well, you are a woman of determination, I'll grant you that. Much like myself in some ways, more's the pity.'' She thrust her lower lip out—the same gesture that Miles used when he was perturbed. Juliana had to fight to keep from smiling. Then the marchioness waggled her beringed fingers toward the door.

"Enough. We'll discuss it later. For now, I'd like to know whatever has happened to Louisa. She was supposed to be keeping herself available.''

"I'll try to find her, if you like.''

"Hmph. Isn't that what I just said?'' She didn't wait for an answer but turned and marched royally out of the room and slammed the door after her.

Juliana leaned against the wall, pressing her bare shoulder against the cool wood as she slowly released her breath. What next? It seemed that every move she made only served to worsen her predicament. Now it seemed inevitable that she would be involved in a political scandal. Was she never to be allowed to live her own life in some semblance of peace?

Still, it occurred to her that the marchioness was not nearly as angry as Juliana would have expected. Or was the worst yet to come? Perhaps she merely held her temper in trust for the moment when they would not be at the mercy of curious guests. Juliana adjusted her gown and patted her hair. This was not the time to think about it. She had promised to find Louisa.

That was easier said than done, Juliana decided after she checked the verandah and the various rooms adjoining the Grand Salon. She had last seen Louisa disappear onto the verandah while Juliana had been dancing with Miles. Could the woman have been so distraught that she sought refuge in the garden to calm her nerves? Martha, who was drinking tea in the kitchen with some of the other servants, confessed after considerable urging that she had noticed her mistress deep in conversation with Don Castillo, a Spanish count. They had been standing near the entrance to the maze not ten minutes ago.

Juliana thanked her but refused Martha's offer of assistance, then slipped out the door to the garden.

She frowned. After dark it was courting scandal to go into the garden unaccompanied by a chaperon, but Juliana noted that the walks were well lit by a series of flambeaux placed strategically at each turn in the path. A few couples, without benefit of chaperon, strolled by. Juliana was tempted to question them about Louisa, but their expressions of amusement left her cold. No doubt they were laughing at her. Well, let them. In a few days' time she would no longer have to worry about her reputation as a member of Polite Society. She would have enough to contend with just to keep herself clothed and fed.

Her thoughts were arrested by the sound of soft whimpering. Juliana felt the hair rise up on the back of her neck. "Louisa?" she called softly. There was no answer. "Louisa, is that you? Where are you?" The whimpering grew louder, and Juliana discovered the source in a secluded gazebo tucked into a niche in the yew hedge.

Louisa was huddled into a corner, her head bowed down to her knees. Her gown, predictably violet, was spread about her in a velvet heap. Juliana touched her softly on the shoulder. "It's Juliana, Louisa. Are you all right? Has someone hurt you?"

Louisa raised tear-reddened eyes. "It's so ghastly. I don't know what I'm going to do." When she straightened, Juliana saw that Louisa's dress was ripped in the front.

Juliana's mouth set in a firm line. "Who did this to you, Louisa? We must tell Miles and have the man apprehended. Was it Don Castillo?"

"No. No! What made you think it was he? You mustn't say anything to Miles, of all people. It—it was an accident. He didn't mean to do it. Truly. It was my fault and mine alone."

"I find that highly suspect. Who are you trying to protect, Louisa? Is it Miles?"

She became visibly agitated. "It is none of your concern, Lady Juliana. Please leave me alone. Go away."

Juliana sat down on the wooden bench that circled the perimeter of the gazebo. Her hands were shaking so that she had to clench them together. "Did Miles do this to you? I must know, Louisa."

"I do not wish to discuss it, and that is final."

Common sense told Juliana that it wasn't like Miles to behave in such a way. If it were the Spanish count, why would Louisa want to protect him? It made more sense that Louisa would defend Miles. Juliana was tortured by doubt, but she struggled to force it from her mind.

"Be sensible, Louisa. You can't go into the house looking like this. Even if you entered through the servants' door, the news would spread like the pox in July."

"Then I shall wait until everyone has gone to bed."

"That could be hours from now. You'd catch your death. Besides, her ladyship is looking for you."

Louisa pressed her hands together under her chin and barely managed to speak. "Wh-what am I g-going to do?"

Juliana stood up. "I think I have an idea." She pulled the silk shawl from her own shoulders and put it around Louisa. "There. Now if we crisscross it like this and bring it around the back and tie it in front, it will cover the damage and look rather decent." She tied it securely, hiding the ends beneath the band, then fluffed the soft pink silk up around Louisa's shoulders. As she did so, Juliana noticed a long gold chain caught up in the fabric of Louisa's chemise. At the end of the chain hung an ornate jeweled locket beautifully designed. Before Juliana could comment on it, Louisa pulled the shawl tight.

"Pink is not my color, but I suppose it will do." She moaned. "But they are sure to see my reddened eyes."

"Not if you hold your fan properly. Once inside the house, you can go to your room and powder your face."

"But they will know that this is your shawl."

Juliana was fast losing patience. "Make up your mind, Louisa. The marchioness will be sending Miles for you if you don't hasten inside. We can go to your room, and I'll help you change into another gown."

She nodded, then got up. While they hurried to the house by a less public route, Louisa questioned her.

"Why would you want to help me, Juliana? We have not been the best of friends since you arrived."

Juliana shot a look at her. The best of friends, indeed! "Suffice to say that there has been enough scandal for one night."

"Scandal? Who? What happened?"

"We've no time for such nonsense. Doubtless you'll hear about it soon enough."

The thought of a scandal served to divert Louisa's mind from her own problems. A short time later they returned to the grand salon, apparently without arousing the suspicion of the guests.

Miles, however, was an exception. He approached Juliana just after Louisa left to attend the marchioness.

"Where in thunder have you been, Juliana? I've nearly driven the servants mad in my search for you."

"I was with Louisa."

"Indeed? That tells me absolutely nothing."

Juliana's heart missed a beat. "Truly? It was my impression that you left her alone in the garden a short half hour ago."

"I haven't so much as stepped my foot off the verandah tonight. Why do you ask?"

She smiled with a warmth that began deep inside her. "I merely wondered. It's nothing to be concerned about."

"Why is it that when you say such things I immediately become concerned?"

Juliana flashed a dazzling smile. "Perhaps you have a suspicious mind, Miles."

"Suspicious? Only where you are concerned. I have learned one thing, my lady, and that is never to take you for granted." He grabbed the ends of his coat in both hands and bowed smartly. "Another thing I've discovered is that dancing puts the sparkle into your eyes. May I suggest we take another turn around the floor?"

"And risk gossip?"

"Devil take the gossips. I can trust you to set them down."

If anything, Juliana's set-to with the Russian nobleman in the bottle-green waistcoat added excitement to the party, and everyone appeared to have a

glorious time. It was late when the last chaise left the
drive and the servants began to put the house back in
order. By the time Juliana retired to her room, she was
grateful that Nadina was on hand to help with the
hooks and buttons and hang the dress in the cedar-
scented armoire. Even then, it was some time before
Juliana could satisfy Nadina's curiosity about everything that had happened. Juliana told her everything,
keeping back only the account of Louisa's unfortunate experience in the garden. Intuition told Juliana
that the fewer people who knew about it the better off
Louisa would be.

CALLING CARDS BEGAN ARRIVING for Juliana early the
next day. Much to her surprise, she received flowers
from half the men she had danced with the previous
night. But the biggest surprise to everyone was when
a mammoth bouquet of pink roses and purple irises
arrived from Alexi Rustegian, whom Juliana continued to think of as the bottle-green waistcoat. Apparently his anger had quickly subsided.

Louisa also received flowers, but there was no card
attached. She looked at the card from the Russian and
made a moue with her mouth. "It was my under-
standing, Juliana, that you had created yet another
scandal with Sir Alexi. Why would he be sending you
flowers? And look. He's asked for the honor of a drive
in Hyde Park on Thursday."

The marchioness impaled Louisa with an imperi-
ous eye. "And just where were you last night when all
that was going on? I had everyone but the scullery
maids searching the house for you."

Louisa blanched. "I had gone for a stroll in the garden."

"With whom? Miles was tête-à-tête with a half-dozen young chits. He could not have been your escort."

"No, it was not Miles. I..." She looked helplessly first at Miles, who was just leaving the room and then at Juliana, who abruptly handed the marchioness a card.

"Can you believe this, Lady Grantsby? That sweet young lieutenant, Roger Beekman, has asked to take me to the park this afternoon. What say you? Do you think I should go? Of course I shall refuse Sir Alexi. I suspect he only wants to get back at me for the insult."

The marchioness frowned. "As for the lieutenant, do as you please, providing you are properly chaperoned. The Russian is another story. You must accept, of course. It will help make amends for your behavior. It's my guess he wants to apologize."

Juliana sighed. "If that is your wish." The marchioness looked surprised at the unexpected obedience. Juliana couldn't help but add, "Besides, the Russian ambassador's nephew may be able to help me find a position. With his connections..."

The marchioness thumped the floor. "Oh, fiddle! Must I employ you myself to keep you from hounding the nob for work?"

"No, your ladyship. It is only that I hate to impose on your hospitality any longer than necessary."

"If you are willing, I would like you to continue to perform the duties of my secretary until she returns in a fortnight. I must insist that you accept a small salary in addition to your lodgings, of course."

"That's very kind of you. Please let me know what work is to be done."

The marchioness motioned her away. "Off with you now. I'll send for you when I need you."

Louisa made haste to depart at the same time. Once outside the room, she grabbed Juliana's arm. "Well, you're a fine one, indeed."

"I beg your pardon?"

"Don't think I'm blind to what you are doing. From the moment you arrived, you've tried to insinuate yourself into this household. Miles may be fooled by your pretty face, but you'll not cozy up to the marchioness for long. You'd be well advised to set about finding a position as soon as possible."

"That is my intention." Juliana studied Louisa's upturned face. "If you would be so good as to release my arm."

Louisa did so, then reached for her lace cap and gave it a vicious tug. "You'll never be accepted here, you know. Granted, the dandies were close on your heels last night at the party, but the women are not fools. You saw how they shunned you."

Juliana was fast losing her temper. "I have nothing to apologize for, but I have a question for you, Louisa. Just who was it you met in the garden last night? Who was the man who tore your gown? Was it Don Castillo?" Juliana asked, remembering the suave, darkly handsome Spaniard she had seen more than once in intimate conversation with Louisa.

"How dare you question me?" Louisa drew herself up sharply, then grabbed her skirt and flounced down the corridor and up the stairs.

As Juliana stood there looking after her, Miles came out of the library. "Egad, what got into Louisa? She's run off like a scared rabbit. Did the two of you have words?"

"No more than usual."

"I take it you saved her hide, and she can't forgive you for it. You slipped one over on the marchioness a moment ago." He chuckled. "Not many people are quite so clever. I'll have to keep a watch on you."

Juliana lifted her chin. "You'd be better advised to keep a watch on Louisa," she said, walking away from him.

He caught her wrist in his firm grasp. "And what is that supposed to mean?"

For a moment Juliana was shaken. His fingers were warm on her arm, but more than the warmth, they sent a tremor of excitement through her. Despite herself she looked up at him until his eyes challenged her with such intensity that she had to turn away.

She ran a moist tongue over her lips. "This family has a penchant for bruising arms."

He swore softly and let her go. "Devil take you, Juliana. You are like a mite under my skin. But I'm glad you waited. I wanted to speak to you alone."

She rubbed her forearm, more to have something to do with her hands than because of any imagined pain. "What is it you want to say?"

"Just this. Despite what Mother says, I don't feel that it is expedient for you to take the air in the park with either the lieutenant or Alexi Rustegian."

Juliana was surprised. "And why not, pray tell?"

"Isn't it obvious? The one is far too young. The other is a renowned womanizer. In your particular position, you must be very careful."

"Of what?"

"Men, of course. Surely you can't be that obtuse. If you wish to ride in the park, I shall be happy to offer my services."

"Indeed? Considering your own reputation as a womanizer, I can't see that you would be an improvement."

He swore competently, then looked apologetic. "Forgive me. In spite of your doubts, you must do as I wish and send your regrets."

"I fear I cannot do that. Her ladyship has made it clear that she thinks I should accept. I fully intend to."

Again he took her wrist in his hand. "Don't anger me, Juliana. I could order you not to go."

"I think not, my lord." She removed his fingers from her arm and, gathering her skirt in her hand, swept past him toward the other end of the corridor. Juliana did not have to look back to know that he remained standing at the door of the library, his hands clenched. Miles was not used to being thwarted.

With only a few exceptions, Juliana sent notes of acceptance to the young bucks who had requested the pleasure of her company. In truth, she had little desire to be courted, but she realized that in order to find suitable employment, she must first convince the ton that she was not a lady of ill repute.

Nadina was happy to be invited to go along as chaperon. Especially when invitations came from young Lieutenant Roger Beekman. It was clear from the moment he saw Nadina that he was smitten. At first, Nadina made a valiant effort to draw back as any good chaperon would do, but neither the lieutenant nor Juliana would permit it, and after a while it seemed as if the roles were reversed, and Juliana had become the chaperon.

Juliana was highly amused, having no personal interest in the young man. He was handsome and every bit the gentleman, but being around the two young people made her feel motherly. When she teased Nadina about her attraction for the young lieutenant and suggested that it might progress beyond a mild flirtation, Nadina was explosive.

"*Non*, madam. *Impossible!* It cannot be. I am merely the orphaned daughter of a French barrister. Even though it is true that I am drawn to Lieutenant Beekman, I have no prospects. He is too far above me." She pushed her heavy hair away from her face. "Besides, it is you who he comes to see."

Juliana laughed. "You don't really believe that."

Seeing the expression on Juliana's face, Nadina joined in her laughter. "You are far too good to me, Lady Juliana."

"Don't thank me. If it were not for you, Nadina, I would be friendless in this big house."

"How can you say that, madam, when Lord Grantsby has eyes for no one but you?"

"Fiddle! He hardly spends any time at all with me."

"It is said he suffers the press of business. His return from the West has opened up new shipping lines to the Americas. Word below-stairs has it that the family business will grow beyond belief."

Juliana turned from her dressing table and looked at Nadina in amazement. "I'm fascinated. How on earth can you know so much about what goes on in the house when we've only been here a short time?"

"I make friends easily." Nadina slanted a sly look across at her. "It is said that Lord Grantsby looks at you with covetous eyes."

Juliana snorted. "Miles merely suffers an occasional touch of nostalgia for the time we spent together at the country house. It is Louisa whom he will eventually offer for. Not me."

"Never. Oh, it is true enough that she pretends to be in love with his lordship, but I can see it in her eyes that she has other kindling on the fire."

Juliana looked quickly at Nadina to see if there was a grain of truth in her words, or if she was merely trying to make Juliana feel better.

Nadina rearranged the combs and brushes into a neat pattern. "But it is true, madam. It is not common knowledge among the downstairs maids, but the upstairs maids have it on good authority."

"That would have to be Martha, Louisa's abigail," Juliana mused aloud.

"I only know it is talked about. Lady Louisa sometimes slips out of her room at night, but no one is privy to her secret."

Juliana knew better than to argue the point. The servant grapevine usually knew what was happening in a household before anyone in the family was even suspicious. Long after she went to bed that night, Juliana thought about it.

IT WAS PERHAPS an hour later. Juliana had just closed her eyes for the tenth time in an effort to fall asleep, but too many thoughts ran willy-nilly through her head. Miles also had retired to his bedchamber shortly after he had returned home. Juliana had heard the soft mumblings of conversation while his manservant looked after him and then left him for the night.

As she lay there, watching the light from the dying fire flicker against the frescoed ceiling, Juliana heard a soft shuffling noise. She tensed. Surely it must be a log shifting in the fireplace. Seconds ticked by, but it remained quiet. She smiled, remembering the stories she and the girls used to tell at Miss Haverstock's Academy. They had outdone each other in an effort to frighten themselves. Experience had taught her to face her fears.

She had no more than closed her eyes when a soft rasping sound of something being drawn across tin or copper made her bolt upright in bed. A mouse? But what mouse could chew through tin? The sound was coming from the fireplace.

Pulling her dressing gown around her, Juliana swung her feet out of bed and crept toward the fireplace. She felt atop the mantel for the gypsy matches that were used to light the lamp. As she was about to lift the globe, a pale beam of light penetrated the room near the floor on the right side of the fireplace. She gasped softly, then put her hand over her mouth to keep from calling out.

"Psst. Juliana. Are you awake?"

"Miles?" Her voice was incredulous. "Is that you? Whatever is the meaning of this? Are you spying on me?"

"Oh, don't be such a prude. I just wanted to talk."

"Through the wall?"

"I'd prefer to be in the same room with you, but I feared you might object."

"Isn't this a bit ridiculous, Miles? I thought you were a rat scuttling around in the woodwork."

"I've been called worse."

"You'll get no argument on that from me, sir."

"Don't be testy."

"What is it you want, Miles? What did you do, have a peephole made in the woodwork so you could watch me?"

"Now who is being ridiculous? If I wanted to watch you, I could find an easier way than crawling around on my hands and knees. Besides, all I can see is your ankles."

She hastily tucked her bare feet under her dressing gown. "I'll thank you to watch your language. Does your mother know you are a Peeping Tom?"

He laughed. "My mother doesn't even know about this peephole. My brother and I fixed it up when we were boys. We used to be sent to our rooms when we misbehaved, but we could still talk to each other without anyone the wiser."

"Oh, yes, I remember Mrs. McGrath saying this suite used to belong to your brother." Juliana had another thought. "And of course, it belonged to Louisa after she was widowed. Did you also waken her in the middle of the night when you wanted to see a woman's ankles?''

He chuckled, and Juliana could almost see the way his moustache twitched and his eyes crinkled in amusement. His voice was deep and husky. "I wonder, could her ladyship be the least bit jealous?''

"Of whom? Louisa certainly has nothing that I want."

"I hope you believe that, but I'm not convinced that you do."

"Either way, it is none of your affair what I think."

"Ah! Have you forgotten that you are under my protection?''

"Some protector! One who spies on his guest in the privacy of her bedchamber. It seems to me I would be well advised to seek other protection. And since you mention it, my lord, you spoke of helping me find a suitable position."

"It isn't easy, considering your limited prospects. Perhaps if you would promise to wear a bag over your head . . ."

Forgetting that she was barefoot, Juliana swung her foot and kicked the cluster of grapes Miles had moved aside to expose the peephole. It was all she could do to keep from cursing as she rubbed her foot to keep it from swelling. "The devil take you, Miles Harcourt. I should have let you die out there in the storm."

"Admit it, Juliana. You wouldn't have missed our time together for the world."

Unfortunately, he was right.

CHAPTER NINE

THE FAMILY HAD already assembled in the breakfast room the following morning when Juliana went downstairs. The marchioness paused in the spearing of a choice morsel of salmon, put down her fork, then lifted her spectacles to her nose.

"Lady Juliana, are you injured? I thought I saw you limping."

"It is nothing, Lady Grantsby. I merely bumped my foot."

Miles was grinning from ear to ear. "What happened, Lady Juliana? Was it a mouse?"

"More likely a rat," Juliana mumbled.

The marchioness thumped her cane. "Speak up, speak up. I do hate having people mumble behind my back."

Miles could hardly contain himself. "It's nothing, Mother. I just reminded Lady Juliana that we are going to attend the opera today."

The marchioness snorted her disapproval at the same time that Juliana shot a spiteful look at Miles.

Louisa, sitting across the table from Miles, appeared completely puzzled by the exchange, but the moment passed and her expression closed. When the marchioness said something to her about going to the silk mercers' on Oxford Street, Louisa didn't seem to hear. The marchioness thumped her cane.

"Well, do we go today or don't we, Louisa?"

Louisa started. "Today? Where?"

"The silk mercers', of course."

"I'm sorry, Mother Harcourt. Today is the meeting of the Ladies' Guild for the Protection of Chimney Sweeps."

"Fiddle. Then I suppose we must wait until tomorrow, but I daresay we must make the decision soon. Rumor has it that the Princess Charlotte will soon announce. If we're to hold a reception here in honor of the betrothal, we must give the seamstresses time to finish our new gowns. I want to go to the plumassier's, too, to select new feathers for my bonnet."

"Yes, indeed, but I have promised Lady Caulder that I will be present at the meeting."

The marchioness placed beringed hands on the arms of the chair and sat stiffly. "It might be prudent to invite Lady Juliana to accompany you to the guild meeting. She and Miles can put off going to the opera until the three of you can go together." She sniffed. "It would be far more appropriate."

Louisa looked alarmed, then immediately caught herself. "Of course, if she wishes to join our select circle, I'm sure she will be welcome."

Miles, standing at the sideboard, just out of his mother's line of vision, made a mischievous face that promised a fair tussle before he would let Juliana out of the promised outing.

A few minutes later, when they were going upstairs, Louisa put her hand on Juliana's arm. "I'd so like to have you go with me to the meeting of the guild, but I fear it is a little late now to add another name to the list. Lady Caulder is so pernickety about last minute changes." Louisa pressed her fingers together in a nervous little gesture, then adjusted her mobcap. "You do understand, don't you, Juliana?"

"Of course. Don't be upset."

Louisa turned sharp eyes on Juliana. "Upset? I'm not upset. Not at all. I merely wanted you to understand so that you could explain it to the marchioness, should she inquire if you accompanied me."

"I understand."

Louisa slowly relaxed. "You'll find the opera ever so much more exciting than our stuffy meeting."

Juliana studied the woman's face. "Louisa, does it not disturb you that Miles plans to escort me?"

Louisa flushed. "Why should it? Miles feels a certain responsibility to you as our houseguest, not to mention the fact that you saved his life." Her voice gathered confidence as she spoke. "I heard tell that he had been asking around the clubs; White's and Almack's, about you. I think he's trying very hard to find employment for you and accommodations—within your limitations, naturally, so that you may live on your own."

Juliana felt her face freeze. "Yes, of course. It's very good of him."

"Nonsense. It is the very least we can do to repay you for saving his life. Miles and I will ever be indebted to you." Louisa smiled so condescendingly that Juliana felt sick to her stomach.

The rest of the morning dragged on interminably. Juliana immersed herself in writing letters for the marchioness, but it was difficult to keep her mind on her work. Any number of times the quill seemed to have a mind of its own, and Juliana had to begin again. Her thoughts kept returning to the afternoon's drive to the King's Theatre in Haymarket, which was the home of the Italian opera.

Did Miles actually plan to flaunt convention by inviting himself to accompany Lieutenant Beekman and herself on the outing? Of course Miles could hardly be aware that the lieutenant was, in truth, paying court to Nadina. For all the attention Juliana received from the rosy-cheeked young man, she might have been one of the lanterns attached to the side of the carriage.

Common sense told Juliana that Miles would not incur his mother's displeasure by taking the air with Juliana while Louisa was otherwise occupied. Without saying so in so many words, the marchioness had made it clear she would do everything in her power to prevent Miles and Juliana from becoming a twosome. Juliana grudgingly admitted that this added credence to Louisa's contention that Miles was expected to marry his brother's widow.

When the appointed hour arrived for the outing, Juliana's nerves were on edge. Even Nadina, who was more patient than any servant Juliana had known, was fast losing her calm.

"Lady Juliana, can you not decide which gown to wear? We have changed three times already."

"I'm sorry. I can't make up my mind. You decide for me."

"The gray velvet would be appropriate."

"But he's seen it before."

"The lieutenant? Surely not, my lady."

Juliana's face turned pink. "I have it. I'll wear the jade green velvet with the white fur trim and the matching muff."

Nadina raised her eyebrows. "But I thought you planned to save it for a special occasion."

Juliana snatched it from the armoire. "Oh, do for heaven's sake credit me with at least making a decision, Nadina."

"*Oui*, madam."

One look at the girl's face revealed her barely controlled amusement. Juliana was about to chastise her but thought better of it. A discussion could only lead to her own embarrassment. For some reason, Nadina seemed to know or suspect the possibility that Miles might accompany the three of them.

When they finally went downstairs to the waiting carriage, Nadina, dressed in a simple gown of slate blue trimmed in burgundy velvet, looked slender and exceedingly feminine. The somber tones served to accentuate her heightened color. Once again Juliana was impressed by her youthful beauty.

The lieutenant looked smart in his neatly tailored uniform with gold braid at the shoulders. He bowed deeply to Juliana, but his eyes dismissed her at once as they traveled on toward Nadina.

Juliana looked around her, but there was no sign of Miles. She felt a stab of pain in her heart. Of course he had done the proper thing by waiting until Louisa could join them, but it was so unlike Miles to be held back by convention. Or was it that he just didn't care enough about Juliana to risk offending his mother by seeing Juliana in public?

The lieutenant was in great spirits as the high-stepping bays drew the chaise onto the cobblestone thoroughfare. He leaned forward, his knees supposedly accidentally brushing against Nadina's knee.

"I've taken it upon myself to order a table at Bartleman's. The day is cool, and I thought you might enjoy tea and cakes."

Nadina blushed prettily. "You should be addressing her ladyship. It is for her to decide."

Juliana, sorely disappointed over Miles's failure to join them, spoke shortly. "My dear Lieutenant. Isn't it time we stopped pretending you are paying court to me? Days ago I realized that it is Nadina whom you wish to see."

Nadina emitted a feeble protest but the lieutenant was boldly set-down. "I say, you can't mean that, my lady. I have nothing but the greatest admiration for you."

Juliana's tone softened. "The truth now, Lieutenant. Is it not Nadina for whom you have eyes?"

He looked at Nadina, who had the good grace to lower her gaze, then he straightened and faced Juliana. "Forgive me, Lady Juliana, but much as I have fought against it, I fear I have become undeniably enamored of Mademoiselle Beaurivage."

"And what do you intend to do about it?"

"That's the devil of it." He looked embarrassed. "Forgive me, your ladyship. The fact is I haven't been able to make any definite plans. In a few weeks I will be leaving for a year's service for the Crown. Until then..." He spread his hands. "I have little in the way of worldly goods on my own and I count it ungentlemanly to offer for her hand under those circumstances."

Nadina looked up quickly. "But I have nothing to offer you as a dowry. I would expect very little in return."

Juliana intervened. "Hush. This is not the time to speak of it. We will talk later, Lieutenant, but I see no reason why you should not see Nadina openly. I confess I tire of playing the cradle robber. You are far too young for me, and I cannot afford to stimulate additional gossip among the beau monde."

His eyes were filled with gratitude. "You are most gracious, Lady Juliana. Nadina and I thank you."

She waved away his thanks and sat back among the cushions, grateful that they couldn't see the tears in her eyes. What she wouldn't give just once to know the kind of love these two young people had for each other.

Although she looked at the passing scenery, Juliana saw little of the park as the carriage moved along the tree-lined street and passed through the gate. When the carriage drew to a halt in front of a bookstore, Juliana leaned forward in surprise.

"Why are we stopping here?"

Before anyone could answer, the lackey had jumped down and lowered the step. An instant later the carriage door opened, and Miles doffed his beaver hat.

"Your ladyship, Mademoiselle Beaurivage, I trust you don't object to carrying another passenger."

Seeing the smiles on Nadina's and the lieutenant's faces, Juliana was taken aback. "Miles, really! You had this planned all along, didn't you?"

"Don't pretend you weren't forewarned, Juliana," he said, taking the seat opposite her and alongside the lieutenant. "I told you last night that I would be joining you."

"You are impossible, sir. I don't know when to take you seriously." A smile dimpled the corners of her mouth as she adjusted a curl beneath her jade bonnet. "You know, of course, that we will be at the mercy of the gossipmongers."

"Does that distress you?"

"Only in that it may injure your family. Your mother and Louisa set great store in keeping the conventions."

He nodded. "Life was simpler at the country house, wasn't it? I miss it."

Her eyes flashed. "You miss the pretense, that's all. You enjoyed playing the brave, seafaring navvy and the bearded country rogue."

"And you, Lady Juliana, enjoyed playing the unemployed lady's maid."

"Ah, but I wasn't playing a game, my lord, for an unemployed lady's maid is precisely what I am."

His voice grew husky, and he pinned her with his gaze. "Juliana, my sweet, you haven't yet begun to respect your true value. You're like a tiny green sapling just emerged from the ground." His gaze swept her delicately molded curves, the slender gloved hands folded demurely in her lap, the carefully contained curls beneath the velvet bonnet. "Juliana, you are beautiful, intelligent, and have more to offer a man than land or goods could account for. Remember that."

Nadina and the lieutenant had stopped talking and were listening with undisguised interest. Juliana was too moved to do or say anything but look properly embarrassed. Then suddenly everyone began talking at once. In the confusion, Nadina reached over and secretly squeezed Juliana's arm.

They stopped first at the tearoom, then drove on to the King's Theatre in Haymarket. Juliana was amazed by the clean lines of the wide, pillared entrance, but she was awestruck when she looked down from the marquis's box in the third tier into the great horseshoe-shaped auditorium that was said to hold over three thousand persons. Miles told her that sometimes the audience overflowed onto the stage.

"I remember once when Madame Rose Didelot, the Parisian danseuse, performed one of her more athletic passages. She swept back her great muscular arms and sent three people sprawling flat onto the floor."

The lieutenant laughed so heartily that it drew the attention of several members of the audience. Juliana noted, with considerable discomfort, that the Duchess of Richmond and her party took turns using a spyglass to observe them.

Juliana quickly snapped open her fan and passed it in front of her face. It was only when the curtain was raised and the music of Mozart began that she was able to draw a breath of relief.

The opera was thrilling to Juliana, who had little experience with such productions, but both the lieutenant and Miles agreed that compared to the great Catalani this latest prima donna was like a tepid milk bath. Juliana enjoyed it, however, but in her heart she knew that it was not just seeing the opera that made her feel such joie de vivre.

Between acts, the audience was abuzz with the rumor that an entourage was present in the royal box. Juliana hoped that the draperies would be opened so that she could get a glimpse of the Prince Regent, but she learned later that it was the Princess Charlotte, along with her soon-to-be fiancé, Prince Leopold of Saxe-Coburg-Saalfield, who were in attendance.

"But I thought the princess was expected to marry the prince of Orange," Juliana said.

Nadina whispered behind her fan. "*Oui*, that is what the Regent had in mind. It was his hope to bring about such an alliance with the future King of the Netherlands. Instead, he must content himself with the son of a German princeling." She laughed. "I cannot say I blame Princess Charlotte. The prince of Orange is said to be slovenly."

The lieutenant leaned forward so as not to be overheard. "I say now, the princess is no gold-plated prize. The Regent has become so sick of trying to find a husband for her that he's cut off her allowance and confined her to Warwich House or Cranbourne Lodge until she makes up her mind. He swears he'll announce her betrothal within the week."

"I wish I could see them," Juliana said, raising her spyglass to look in the direction of the royal box.

Miles patted her hand. "Don't fret. You will have an opportunity to make your curtsy when we have the reception for them at Grantsby Hall."

Juliana made a face. "By then I shall have taken up residence in my own apartments."

A secretive smile played across Miles's face. "I doubt that you will be leaving us so soon, Lady Juliana. If I were you, I would be concentrating my thoughts on what to wear to the grand ball."

LATER, AS SHE LAY under the canopied bed in her bedchamber, Juliana remembered what he had said. The reception, if the Regent had his way about announcing a betrothal, was expected to take place within the next month. Was it conceivable that she would still be in residence here?

She was torn between the need to get on with her life, to have some direction, and the very strong desire to remain close to Miles. Although she had met quite a number of influential people in the past week, Juliana was no closer to securing a position than she had been when she arrived. Was it true, as Louisa had said, that Miles was attempting to find suitable employment for her? She mentally chastised herself for not forcing him to tell the truth when she had the chance.

But did she really want to know? If truth be told, she was not eager to become slave to some woman of disagreeable temperament. She rolled onto her side and watched the dying embers in the fireplace. If she were as anxious to become self-sufficient as she had given the marchioness to believe, then, Juliana admitted, she should have placed a position-wanted notice in the newspaper. It was the proper thing to do, rather than remain a burden to the Harcourt family. Besides, to linger on in the household would only serve to make the parting more difficult. Miles belonged to Louisa, or would one day soon. Juliana knew she must begin to accept it as fact.

The mere thought of it brought tears to her eyes, and she blinked rapidly, dabbing at her face with the edge of her satin comforter.

At first she thought the sound she heard was her own sniffling, but then she recognized the metallic scrape of the secret panel at the foot of the fireplace.

Miles! She sat up in bed and studied the wide beam of light that penetrated the opening. What did he want now? Wouldn't it be better to pretend she was asleep?

"Juliana." His voice was hardly audible in the velvet darkness that had seemed to grow darker in contrast to the single shaft of light. "Juliana," he repeated, this time so loudly that she feared he might waken Nadina in the next room. Juliana swung her feet out of bed and ran to the fireplace, pulling a quilt around her on the way.

"Miles, do be still. What is it you want? This is scandalous behavior, talking through the wall like two children."

"Not so scandalous. Nadina tells me you still have Mrs. Frobisher as our chaperon."

Juliana looked at the rag doll she had carried with her from the country house. It was sprawled on the bed, its odious red hair in rakish disorder. "Miles, you are impossible." She giggled despite her attempt to remain serious.

"Did I waken you?"

"No. I couldn't sleep."

"Neither could I. Talk to me."

She laughed, seeing in her mind's eye the little boy look on his face. "What is it you want, Miles, a bedtime story? Are you afraid to fall asleep in the dark?"

"Sleep is a waste of time."

"In truth, I was just thinking about you," she admitted.

"What an uncanny coincidence. You've hardly left my thoughts all day."

"No doubt you've been racking your brain in order to help me find a position." She dropped to the floor and leaned against the carved wood that decorated the fireplace. The swansdown quilt covered her from her chin to her feet. "Tell me, Miles," she continued. "Have you found anyone who might take me on as a companion or governess?"

He swore softly. "It is only out of a sincere regard for your well-being that I have made inquiries about you. You must accept my word, Juliana. There are a dozen or more young fops and aging dandies who would accept you in either category, but I doubt that you would agree to accept the duties. It seems you are considered something of a fallen woman by the ladies of Polite Society. My fault, I fear."

"Why do you say that?"

He chuckled softly. "Has it not occurred to you, my sweet Juliana, that in my position I could have made arrangements much sooner to have us rescued from the country house?''

"But you were weak."

He laughed. "Morally weak, perhaps. The time I spent alone with you was one of the most satisfying interludes I have enjoyed in my entire life. Had I been a gentleman, I would have arranged for one of the village women to act as chaperon. Instead, I chose to have you all to myself."

"You are despicable, you know that, Miles?" She had intended it to be a cutting remark, but somehow the edges of it were dulled by the warmth in her voice.

"So you have told me on several occasions."

Juliana rested her chin on her knees. "Why do you admit to it now? I mean the business about the chaperon?"

"I wanted to be honest with you."

Hearing the huskiness in his voice, she hugged her knees closer. "I'm grateful for that, at least." She waited for him to say something, but silence filled the room like air expanding a huge balloon.

She felt compelled to continue. "Since you mention honesty, Miles, tell me one thing. Is it true that your family expects you to marry Louisa now that your brother is dead? Or is this something dreamed up by your mother and Louisa to force us to—to avoid creating another scandal?"

Juliana could almost see his lower lip thrust out as he considered his answer. He moved, and she could hear him lean back against the wall directly opposite hers. He seemed reluctant to answer, and when he did, his voice was heavy and cold.

"It has been the custom in past generations of our family for the surviving brother to take on the responsibilities of the deceased."

"I see. That was my impression."

"It doesn't have to be that way, Juliana."

"I doubt that the marchioness will agree with you. From what I understand, Louisa stands to inherit a considerable fortune when her father dies. The alliance would, in fact, unite two of the largest shipping companies in Britain, a merger that would challenge the supremacy of The East India Company. Is that not correct?"

"It's true." His voice was sober as he answered.

"Then what more is there to say?"

"That money isn't everything. That love forms a stronger bond than gold."

"Platitudes, Miles. Besides, there has been no talk of love."

"An oversight, I assure you. Or perhaps I simply lacked the courage."

Juliana's fingers were chilled, and she reached one hand down to the ribbon of light. Dust motes danced when she disturbed the air. She turned her hand, cupping the light in her palm, then spreading her fingers to make shadow pictures on the floor. She imagined the light with a life of its own; a living entity linking his warmth with hers.

The silence grew heavy. She wanted to say something frothy and frivolous, but the thickness in her throat prevented her from speaking.

What did he mean by lack of courage? Had he been his own master for so long that he feared losing his freedom by taking a wife? Or was he simply afraid to go against his mother's wishes? Neither explanation was acceptable.

It was difficult for her to reconcile the Miles of the country house with the Miles she had come to know in London. One, the navvy rogue who had teased and delighted her. The other, the marquis, a man of power who strongly influenced worldwide commerce as well as politics.

One man, with a many-faceted personality. The most fascinating man she had ever met. And unfortunately for her peace of mind, she had fallen irrevocably in love with him.

CHAPTER TEN

IT WAS TWO DAYS LATER when the blue-and-gold liveried page arrived with a message bearing the royal crest. Lady Grantsby, waving the heavily embossed letter in her hand, swept triumphantly into the library where Juliana was writing letters. Louisa, seated in a far corner, was reading *Emma*, by Jane Austen, a fact that she hurriedly concealed from the marchioness who strongly disapproved of novels as a pandering to one's baser instincts.

"It's done," the marchioness crowed. "The Crown has accepted the offer of the German prince. Princess Charlotte has set May second for the wedding ceremony." Lady Grantsby suddenly remembered her cane, which she had been brandishing like a scepter, and she leaned her weight against it. "Furthermore, they have graciously accepted my offer to give a party in their honor here at Grantsby Hall in three weeks' time."

Louisa clapped her hands. "Magnificent! We must have beaten everyone to the bid. Lady Jersey will be green with envy." Louisa turned pensive for a moment, then brightened. "She will doubtless give a rout to celebrate the nuptials, but for us to be the first! I can scarcely believe it."

The marchioness perched her lorgnette on the end of her nose. "Lady Juliana, am I wrong, or do I detect a decided lack of enthusiasm?"

"It is only that I have been away from such festivities for so many years. My husband rarely asked me to accompany him when he went to London, so my social obligations were somewhat limited to Dorset."

"How provincial," Louisa murmured.

"On the contrary." Juliana felt compelled to protest. "I find country life quite stimulating. But one does lose touch with the comings and goings at court."

Lady Grantsby settled herself gracefully into a Queen Anne chair, her spine as stiff as her cane. "Suffice it to say that in London one must keep up, or one is left by the wayside. Juliana, I will expect you to begin at once on the invitations. We have much to do to prepare for the reception." She peered across at Louisa, turning her body instead of her head.

"Louisa, I'll want you to supervise the turnout of the grand salon. Everything must come down for a shake out: the draperies, the tapestries. The crystal chandelier must be polished, the floors and woodwork hand-rubbed with beeswax."

Louisa looked irritated. "Shouldn't it be up to Mrs. McGrath to supervise the cleaning? I have my committees to attend."

"Nonsense! Nothing is more important than setting the house to rights for the Royal Family."

"Will the Princess Caroline be in attendance?" Juliana asked, referring to Princess Charlotte's mother, the wife of the Regent.

Both Louisa and the marchioness snorted. Louisa gave Juliana a "poor little you" look.

"Surely you must be aware that Princess Caroline and the Regent are at sword's point, as they have been almost since the beginning. It is just a question of time and the judgment of Parliament until he discards her permanently."

The marchioness nodded. "Princess Caroline could never abide Prinny's open attraction for Lady Hertford. But admittedly, although the populace is sympathetic toward Princess Caroline, she has never been a credit to the Crown. God forbid that she should ever succeed the queen."

They were discussing the latest of Princess Caroline's escapades when Miles came into the library. He bowed to them, then went to stand in the curve of the bay window.

"Miles, have you heard the news?" his mother asked.

"How could I not? There's not a lackey or scullery maid in the house who isn't agog with the talk about the party."

Louisa beamed. "All of London will be begging for an invitation. Isn't it too, too exciting? I could just swoon."

The marchioness waggled her fingers. "This is no time to succumb to the vapors, Louisa. Miles, I must have a list of those whom you wish to invite. I especially want to know which persons you will expect to stay overnight."

He went to the desk and drew out paper and a pen. "That shouldn't be too difficult. There are perhaps four or five families who will need lodgings because of the distance they have to travel. I count the Duke and Duchess of Heatherford, the Viscount and Viscountess of Glenbrook, the Baron and Baroness Montland. I know you enjoy their company, and they have been such good friends of the family."

His lower lip protruded as he mentally ticked off the names. "Of course, we must invite Sir Hilary Gordon and the Earl of Fordyce to spend the night. They are no great friends of mine, but for reasons of my own, I find it politically expedient." His voice continued, but Juliana heard no more. Her heart nearly stopped beating.

Miles paused midsentence. "What is it, Juliana? Are you ill? You've suddenly turned pale as a ghost."

"Did...did I understand you correctly? Did you mention the Earl of Fordyce?"

"Indeed. He is to be one of our houseguests."

"How could you, Miles? Surely you don't expect me to remain under the same roof as him? You can't have forgotten that the earl was the man responsible for the death of my husband."

"You must trust me, Juliana. Until you have proof..."

Her voice rose. "Of course I don't have proof. If I did, I wouldn't have been turned out of my own home like a back-street beggar. But I know that he was the man who hired those ruffians to murder my husband and steal the deed to our holdings."

Louisa looked bored. "That's absurd. The earl is an exceedingly rich man. Why would he have to stoop to such treachery?"

"Maybe that's how he remains rich," Juliana countered. "It is a well-known fact that he has a penchant for gambling. Few gamblers keep their money for long, yet the earl continues to spend as if he had a direct line to the palace vaults."

The marchioness thumped her cane on the floor. "Be that as it may, we cannot insult the earl by failing to invite him and his entourage." She swiveled to face Juliana. "I can sympathize with your anger, my dear, but you must learn to adapt. The house is large enough that you need not fear a personal encounter with the earl. I shall see to it that he does not harm you in any way."

Miles threw his head back and laughed. "And who is to protect the earl, Mother? You have not seen Juliana when she is angry. God help the man if he crosses her."

The marchioness folded her hands regally across her cane. "I venture we have nothing to fear from her ladyship. You must remember, Miles, that although Juliana is presently without funds, she is still a lady and will most certainly behave like one."

Miles half covered his mouth with his hand and murmured toward Juliana, "She'll change that tune when she sees you in action."

Juliana gave him a look intended to wither. "And you, my lord, had best see that the earl remains on the opposite side of the house from me, or I warrant I'll not be held responsible for his safety—or yours."

The marchioness thumped the floor. "Speak up, speak up, I tell you. Now enough of this idle discussion. Where must we begin?"

Juliana forced her anger to subside as she pulled a pad of paper from a cubbyhole in the desk and prepared to work. "I suppose the invitations must come first, Lady Grantsby."

Louisa made a big show of looking at the ornate gold ormolu clock atop the fireplace mantel. "Oh, dear, I must leave soon for my committee meeting." She turned to a footman near the door. "See that Martha, my abigail, is sent to my rooms at once to help me dress."

When she was gone, the marchioness turned to Juliana. "I don't recall Louisa mentioning a meeting of her committee today. Do you know exactly which group she is attending?"

Juliana shook her head. "I'm sorry, Lady Grantsby. I only know that the committees are time-consuming. Louisa works very hard for her charities."

"Hmph. We could use a little of her charity in turning out the grand salon. As for you, Miles, you'll want to supervise the groundskeeper and see to it that the stables are made ready for the additional horses and carriages."

He looked over at Juliana and gave a conspiratorial wink. The marchioness must have caught it out of the corner of her eye because she looked speculatively at first one and then the other. Juliana felt the color rise up in her face, and she bent quickly to lift the cover of the inkstand.

The moment passed, and shortly the marchioness was up to her glory in regimenting the plans for the grand ball.

LATER THAT NIGHT in her room, Juliana was nestled in her quilt on the floor beside the peephole at the base of the fireplace. It was good to have someone to talk to in the loneliness of the darkened room. And what did it matter? No one was the wiser. She had begun to look forward to hearing the metallic scrape that meant Miles was on the other side of the wall waiting to talk to her.

It occurred to her more than once that unlike most gentlemen of the ton who would have gone to White's or Brook's Club for an evening of hazard, Miles seemed to enjoy spending his secret hour with her. She mentally chastised herself. He wasn't really with her. There was always the safety of a solid wall between them to satisfy convention.

Still, there had been a time when she had pressed her hands opposite the place where she knew he must be resting his shoulder, and Juliana could have sworn she felt the heat of his body. The sudden warmth that had flooded her veins startled her, and she had pulled back, pressing her hands against her face. After that for two nights she had failed to respond to Miles's voice when the beam of light penetrated her room. He had questioned her about it later, but she told him she must have fallen asleep. He didn't believe her. She wasn't good at dissembling.

It was odd how Miles affected her. He had asked her to trust him. It was a simple matter when he was nearby, but when he was away, all her doubts seemed to magnify into one great lump in the pit of her stomach. But she needed to trust him. Needed his teasing laughter. Needed the sound of his voice. And so she gave way to the inevitable and responded to the scrape of the secret peephole.

In truth, those secret hours alone with Miles were the high point of her day. Now, she closed her eyes and leaned her head back against the wall, feeling tired yet oddly at peace with herself.

"Is it always like this in London society, Miles? Don't they ever tire of parties and routs?"

"Apparently not. At least among the bon ton. As for myself, I have lived in America and the Indies for so long that I have not been a part of the social scene until recently."

"Maybe that's why you seem so different from other men," she mused aloud.

"Different? In what way?"

She considered for a moment. There was no way she could tell him that she found him more intelligent, more mature, more honorable, and above all, more fascinating than any man she had ever met. To do so would give him the advantage over her.

She chewed her lip for a few seconds before she answered. "For one thing, Miles, I consider you less foppish."

He laughed. "Is that a polite way of telling me that I am not fashionably dressed, or is it a hint that you don't find me appealing in manly ways?"

"I'll warrant your self-esteem makes up for whatever else you lack. Don't expect me to add to it, Miles. Suffice it to say that you have seen fit to supervise the running of the family shipping business while most men of means fritter away their lives at the gambling tables or houses of ill repute."

"It was no sacrifice, I assure you. I have never professed an interest in gambling."

She was waiting for the other shoe to fall, but he remained silent. When she could stand it no more, she spoke. "And?"

His voice sounded amused. "And what?"

"Lord Grantsby," she said in an outraged voice, "you have omitted one very important statement."

"What was that?"

"You know very well what I'm talking about. But never mind. I think I already know the answer." She fidgeted, trying to find a comfortable position on the hard floor. "Sometimes, Miles, more is said by what is left unsaid, than by what is actually put into words."

"Profound, I'm sure. But what does it actually mean?"

She compressed her lips. "It means that this conversation is going nowhere." She reached over to the fireplace and slid the carved bunch of grapes into place over the panel, closing out the light as well as Miles's voice. An instant later the panel slid open again.

"Don't run away from me like that, Juliana."

"Then don't bedevil me."

"My apologies, madam. What is it you want from me? Are you asking about how many women I have known?"

"Miles! Must you be so outspoken?"

"You haven't answered my question."

Juliana's irritation was reflected in her voice. "I have no wish to delve into your personal life. What you do is no concern of mine."

"I consider that a partial truth. If you must know, I am not a saint, Juliana, but on the reverse side of the coin, I do not frequent bawdy houses, nor do I keep a mistress tucked away in a pied-à-terre.''

She smiled, warmed by the sincerity in his voice. "Admirable, indeed, but doesn't it worry you that some people might think you a bit light-footed, considering that you are getting along in years and have yet to take a bride?"

"Egad!" he exclaimed. "Tell me that you are one of those unfortunates who believe such rubbish, Juliana. I would delight in having an excuse to come over there and prove otherwise."

"No thank you, sir. I will take you at your word."

"Coward."

She smiled. It was several moments before either of them spoke. She was lost in musing on what such an encounter might be like. Then Miles broke into her splendid fantasy.

"But you do have a point, Juliana. Indeed, I've thought much about it since coming home to England. Now that I have the family business well in hand, I think the time is fast approaching for me to take a bride."

Juliana felt her mouth go dry. She was struggling to find an appropriate answer when a faint knock sounded on the door. At first she thought it came from her own sitting room, but Miles swore softly.

"I must go. There is someone at my door. Good night, Juliana." He closed the peephole without waiting for her response.

Juliana listened for a few minutes to the soft murmur of voices from the opposite side of the wall. It was impossible to determine what was being said, or indeed, whether it was a man or a woman with whom Miles was speaking. The temptation to open the peephole was agonizing, but she had never been the one to initiate their secret conversations, and neither would she stoop so low as to spy on Miles under any circumstances.

But the question lingered in her mind until she finally fell asleep. It was perhaps two hours later when she heard a noise in the hallway. Was it the soft closing of a door? Forgetting her resolve not to spy, she scurried out of bed and opened her sitting room door just wide enough so that she could see into the dimly lit corridor.

It was Louisa. There was no doubt in Juliana's mind because when Juliana's eyes adjusted to the light, Louisa was just abreast of the door. Their eyes met for one sickening moment. Neither of them spoke, but Juliana eased the door shut and leaned her head against her arm.

Miles, the swine, had lied to her! He and Louisa had apparently not waited until their expected betrothal to sample the delights of marriage.

The pain of knowing the truth was so great that she could hardly crawl back into bed. Even then, sleep was beyond question. No longer could she entertain dreams, however fragile, that one day Miles might offer for her.

The reality of the situation was as real as bathing in ice water. She must begin at once to make plans to leave Grantsby Hall. Tomorrow she would place an advertisement in the positions-wanted section of the newspaper. The marchioness would be furious, of course, so Juliana would have to do it secretly.

When morning finally came, she felt a little better despite her lack of sleep. Hard work and a definite purpose in mind were great healers. The marchioness saw to it that everyone was kept busy from the moment breakfast was over until well after midday.

It was small consolation that when Nadina remarked upon the circles under Juliana's eyes, the outspoken abigail mentioned that Lady Louisa looked far worse. As a kindly Providence would have it, Juliana didn't have to face Louisa alone, and no mention was made of her midnight tryst.

Miles, on the other hand, appeared refreshed and ready to cope with the affairs of the estate. Juliana went out of her way to avoid talking to him. If he noticed her sudden coolness, he made no mention of it. Fortunately they were too busy to be left alone together even once during the morning.

In the afternoon, Juliana made arrangements to be taken to Oxford Street to shop for some fabric to be made into a gown for the Princess Ball. In truth, her real reason for going out was to place the notice in the *Morning Post*. She had written it carefully: "Noblewoman of virtue and intelligence seeks employment as a governess..." The notice did not reveal her name but asked interested parties to respond by a letter of inquiry to the *Post*.

The very anonymity of it would protect her from unscrupulous persons, as well as save the Harcourt family from undue gossip.

Nadina, who had accompanied Juliana to the newspaper office, was not at all impressed with Juliana's sense of urgency.

"I do not understand you at all, madam. I thought English ladies of quality were content to be taken care of."

"Is that what the other women you worked for were like?"

Nadina raised her eyes heavenward. "*Mon Dieu.* If they could have found someone to lift the spoons to their mouths, they would have waited to be fed. But you, madam, are different, though perhaps not too perceptive." Nadina looked momentarily contrite before she continued.

"There is a place for you here in the Harcourt family. I can see it in his eyes that his lordship will soon offer for you."

Juliana felt a knot begin to tighten in her stomach. "It is true that he is thinking seriously of marriage, but I'm afraid he has another woman in mind."

"Never!"

Juliana could not bear to discuss it. She spoke rather abruptly to Nadina, regretting it even as she did so, but it put an end to the conversation. Later, Juliana tried to make it up to Nadina by selecting some pink silk roses at the plumassier's with which to decorate her gray velvet bonnet. Nadina accepted them graciously but not with her usual delight in such things.

Juliana's funds were dwindling rapidly, and she was unable to find anything that pleased her. Truthfully, she was not even remotely interested in what to wear to the Princess Ball. Nadina was appalled.

"Are you so destitute that you cannot afford to buy the Chinese blue silk? *Mon Dieu!* Why did I let you buy the roses?"

"Don't be silly. The little they cost would not have been enough to cover the cost of the dress material. Besides, I didn't want it."

There were tears in Nadina's eyes. "You are far too good to me, madam. I wish I could serve you better."

"You deserve much more than I could ever do for you, Nadina. I only wish there was some way I could promise to take you with me when I leave. You would do well, you know, to start looking around for a permanent position. Even when I do find work, it will pay scarcely enough to keep me. There is no way I could afford to pay you anything."

Nadina shrugged. "Tomorrow will take care of itself."

When they arrived back at Grantsby Hall, the butler advised Juliana that a gentleman was waiting to see her.

She let the footman take her cloak and bonnet, then straightened up her hair and followed him to the library. Lieutenant Roger Beekman rose when the butler announced Juliana.

"Lady Juliana, please forgive this intrusion, but it is a matter of no small importance."

She motioned him to a brocade settee. "Please sit down, Lieutenant Beekman." Then, sitting opposite him, Juliana folded her hands in her lap. "You look distraught. May I ring for tea?"

He shook his head. "No I . . . Not for me, Lady Juliana, unless you prefer . . ." he said, his nervousness obvious in the way he gripped the arm of the settee.

Juliana touched his arm. "Roger. Please tell me what is wrong."

"Oh, I say. Nothing's wrong, my lady. At least not yet. I've come to ask your blessing."

Juliana was genuinely confused. "My blessing?"

"Yes. It's like this. I have finally gotten up the courage to offer for Mademoiselle Nadina's hand in marriage. Since she has no family—" he shrugged "—there is no one else to ask."

He leaned forward, his cheeks rosy with anticipation and an earnest desire to plead his case. "The worst of it is that I am about to be sent to France for a few weeks, and I can't bear to leave without her promise to marry me. What do you think, Lady Juliana? May we have your permission?"

Juliana tried to hide her smile. She questioned him in all seriousness for several minutes, then determined that he was as much ready for marriage as most young men.

"And what about your family? Will they approve? Nadina is not highborn, you know. Her father was a barrister, but as you say, he is no longer alive and there can be no dowry."

"I have already received my father's blessing. He trusts my judgment."

"Then can I do less, Roger? Of course you have my blessing. I've grown very fond of Nadina. I trust you to take good care of her."

His eyes were moist. "Thank you. Thank you, my lady. May I see her now? I want to be first to tell her the good news."

Juliana rang for the butler, and a footman was sent to fetch Nadina, who was apparently waiting less than a dozen feet down the hall.

JULIANA BEGGED to be excused from dinner that night on the pretext of a slight sore throat. The marchioness ordered a tureen of soup and a cold collation sent to her room. Nadina brought another tray from back stairs, and they dined together on a table set next to the fireplace in Juliana's bedroom.

They talked for some time about Nadina's betrothal, and for the first time that day Juliana's spirits lifted.

Nadina watched Juliana take a sip of tea, then start to nibble an apricot tart only to put it down.

"*Oui*, you do have a touch of sore throat, don't you. I thought it was merely an excuse to avoid dining with Lady Louisa."

"It's nothing. More a case of nerves than anything else."

"Perhaps I should ask the maid to bring more wood for the fire." She grinned slyly. "Either that, or madam had best use two quilts when she sits on the floor next to the fireplace tonight."

Juliana couldn't hide her shock. "You know? You know about the—" she motioned to the covered peephole.

"*Oui*. I know." Nadina's face was wreathed in smiles. "I have known all along, but I have told no one."

Juliana held the cup of tea so tightly that she thought for a moment it might shatter. "Anyway, it's over. I'll not be playing that game again."

CHAPTER ELEVEN

JULIANA MEANT IT when she told Nadina that she was finished with Miles. In truth, had there ever been anything between them but a prickly sort of friendship? Except in a jesting way, Miles had never stepped beyond the limits of propriety imposed by society. In no way could she pretend that he had tried to force himself on her or that he had given any indication that he might fall in love with her.

But Nadina wasn't to be put off. She protested that her instincts were never wrong when it came to men. She was certain that Miles was strongly attracted to Juliana.

A part of Juliana wanted to believe her but common sense prevailed. Whether it was to keep Miles from opening the peephole, or to keep herself from hoping that he would do so, Juliana moved a chaise longue close to the fireplace. It blocked the peephole, making it impossible to determine whether or not it was open.

It was late when Nadina ran out of energy and retired to her own room. Juliana was bone weary from the long day and the thought of similar days stretching out ahead of her. She knew in her heart it wasn't the work that bothered her. It was the thought of all those endless years without Miles.

If he tried to open the peephole that night, Juliana was unaware of it. She lay on her side, refusing to turn in the direction of the fireplace until she fell asleep.

In spite of her overwhelming sadness, the days sped by quickly. Juliana had finished the last of the invitations and the messengers had delivered them almost before the ink was dry. After that, there were dozens of place cards to print in Juliana's fine Carolingian script.

Much to the pleasure of the marchioness, Louisa, too, managed to do her share of the work in preparation for the Princess Ball. Four days before the date set for the festivities, all the responses were in hand, and there were no refusals.

Juliana's hope that the Earl of Fordyce would send his regrets vanished when she recognized his black and red crest, depicting a charging bull on a shield of crossed swords.

She was not a person to whom hate came easily, but in his case she made an exception. Not that her husband had been without blame. Juliana saw gambling as a pastime of the indolent, the weak. Cedric could just as easily have lost everything, but as Dame Fortune would have it, he had won. This she had discovered by talking to a serving maid who had been privy to the wagers. Unfortunately for Juliana, the servant was sent away shortly afterward.

Unwilling to take the gentlemanly way out and honor the bet that would have given Cedric clear title to an importing business owned by the earl, the Earl of Fordyce had chosen to hire cutthroats to waylay Cedric in the mews behind the gambling house. They had beaten Cedric until he was dead, then stole back the title to the business, along with the deed to Cedric's estate, which he had placed as security against his wager.

Powerful as he was, no one would speak out against the earl. Juliana sank down wearily in the chair and held the crested stationery in her shaking hands. And now she would see him again. Could she manage to get through the festivities without falling apart?

The marchioness, her cane thumping along the floor, still managed to look regal as she came into the room, her magnificent coronet of hair covered now with a mobcap.

"Oh, there you are, Lady Juliana. What is it? You look peaky."

Juliana rose and curtsied. Without speaking, she handed the letter to the marchioness, who sniffed. "Well, it should come as no surprise to you, my dear. Did you think he would send his regrets rather than appear at a party for the royal family?" Apparently the question was too ridiculous to require an answer because she settled herself in a straight chair and continued.

"What have you decided to wear for the ball?"

"I have not come to a decision. It really doesn't matter. I shall find something among my wardrobe."

"Great lackaday! You must realize that our houseguests will begin arriving tomorrow, and the ball is the day after. I cannot comprehend your disinterest."

"I'm sorry, your ladyship. I've tried to do my part, but you must know that my own future is uppermost in my mind."

"Yes, I've heard about the notice in the newspaper. I instructed the editor to cancel it."

Juliana was appalled. "You what? You had no right, Lady Grantsby. I'm shocked by your insensitivity to my problem."

"Nonsense. I simply won't have you taken in by any old Peter or Tom who might have the manners and morals of a goat." She thumped her cane to emphasize her point. "One thing at a time, me gal. Let's get this ball together, and then we'll find something suitable for you to do. You must, after all, remember your position."

Juliana knew better than to argue. She pressed her lips together, as if to hold back the words, then sighed. "One thing I would like to know, if you would be so good. Who told you about my notice in the newspaper? Was it Nadina?"

"Oh, dear me, no. I wouldn't stoop to questioning your abigail. Besides, she is beyond bribery. Suffice it to say that I have my sources of information. There is little that gets past me, my dear. Do remember that." The marchioness fitted her lorgnette onto the end of her nose.

"I was right, wasn't I? You do look overly tired. I want you to take some time to yourself this afternoon. Go for a drive in the park with Sir Alexi or that nice young lieutenant."

Juliana was surprised. The marchioness had never been impressed by Alexi, though he had gone out of his way to be cordial. The few times Juliana had permitted him to call on her, both the marchioness and Miles were critical. But this sounded more like an order than a suggestion.

"As it happens, Sir Alexi has begged permission to call today. He's been asking to take me to Vauxhall Gardens," she mused aloud. "It might be good to get away from the tension of the house for a few hours. I believe I will take the air with him this afternoon, Lady Grantsby, if you are sure you don't need me."

"Go along with you now. Wear something warm and pretty. It will put some color in your cheeks." She adjusted her snow-white fichu, which was fastened in place by a ruby brooch.

"I declare, you young people have no stamina. Miles has not stood up to the task of getting the house in order as I expected he would. I grant you, he has worked like a slavey, but his good nature has suffered for it. I'd advise you not to cross swords with him for the next few days."

Juliana thanked her and then went upstairs to summon Nadina to lay out their clothing for the afternoon's outing.

SIR ALEXI PREENED like a peacock when Juliana said that she would enjoy a drive. The weather was balmy for January, and he had a new park phaeton with a fine pair of blooded bays he wanted to show off. Instead of Vauxhall Garden, they decided to drive through Regents Park, which would be almost deserted at this particular time.

Although the Russian was exceedingly handsome in a delicate way and was known to be very wealthy, Juliana had little interest in cultivating anything beyond a casual friendship. Given other circumstances, she would have refused him, but considering that she was looking for work, she felt well advised not to burn any bridges.

As luck would have it, some inefficient lackey had failed to properly tighten a bolt on the new carriage. As they were rounding a curve at a fairly fast clip, one of the tongues pulled loose, causing the carriage to slew sideways. The horses were terrified, though the driver managed to calm them, but it was two hours before they were able to reattach the tongue to the carriage.

When Sir Alexi finally delivered Juliana and Nadina safely back to Grantsby Hall, the marchioness, Louisa and Miles, were all waiting impatiently in the library.

Juliana stopped there first to offer her apologies before she went upstairs to change her clothing. Miles was in a towering rage.

"Well, it is about time you decided to put in an appearance, Lady Juliana. Where in God's good name have you been all afternoon?"

"I—"

"We have been combing the town for you and that cad, Alexi Rustegian. I demand you give an accounting."

"You have no right to speak that way about Sir Alexi. His behavior is above reproach. As to your question, we went to Vauxhall Garden—"

Miles interrupted before she could finish. "The devil you did. I personally searched for you there. I even searched the maze."

The marchioness fluttered her fan in front of her face. "Miles, do calm down. There's nothing to be gained by attacking Juliana in such a way."

He paced across the room, his boots making a harsh noise between the expensive rugs that were scattered at random on the polished oak floor.

"You amaze me, Mother. You, who are so strict about keeping the rules of Polite Society. How can you sit there and defend her when you know that she is keeping company with a scoundrel? That womanizer! Egad. He is beneath contempt."

Milcs went back to stand in front of Juliana. His hands were on his hips, his legs spread wide, accentuating his trim muscular calves.

"I'm waiting to hear from you, Lady Juliana. Where were you? What kind of mischief have you contrived to involve us in this time?"

Juliana was not used to being confronted in such a way. She was still too much the nobelwoman to allow someone to treat her like an indentured servant. She slowly untied her bonnet and held it in her two hands, contemplating him as calmly as her thudding heart would permit.

"It was as I told you, your lordship. The three of us, Sir Alexi, Nadina and myself, went to Vauxhall Gardens and—"

He swore competently, causing Louisa to gasp and his mother to frown.

Juliana straightened. "I'll thank you to watch your language, sir. I regret that my late return has caused you concern, but I do not see the necessity of keeping you informed of my whereabouts." She threaded the bonnet ribbon through her shaking fingers. "When you so noisily interrupted me, I was about to tell you that we tired of Vauxhall Gardens after a few minutes and decided to take Sir Alexi's new park phaeton for a drive. In Regents Park we had a minor accident, which took some time to repair."

The color slowly came back into Miles face. "Do you swear to this?"

A rush of anger threatened to choke Juliana. She flung her bonnet on the floor in a sudden fit of temper. "No, I most certainly do not swear to it. I have stated very clearly what happened. That should be sufficient."

Louisa, who had leaned forward so as to not miss a word, straightened and laced her fingers together. "I thought as much. You are certain to bring disgrace on this family. I warned her ladyship so repeatedly." She raised her eyes heavenward. "Great lackaday. Alexi Rustegian, of all men. He is a professional charmer, and a foreigner, as well."

Miles turned to look at the marchioness, who saw his expression of helplessness. She smiled and shrugged. "If I were you, Miles, I would let it go at that for now."

Miles glared. "If we can't expect an apology, then the least her ladyship can do is to vow not to see the Russian again."

"I have no intention of making such a promise. You have no control over me, sir, except for those things that fall within the constraints of the household. There is no reason there should be any gossip, unless you yourself spread stories that have no basis in fact."

The marchioness thumped her cane. "None of us can say that any harm has been done. Suppose we cool our tempers with a glass of sherry?" She reached for a bell, and its silver tinkle sounded sweet in the overcharged air.

Miles didn't stay long enough for the sherry to be served. Without another word he stormed out of the library, and they heard the door to the service wing slam shut. Louisa made a hurried curtsy to the marchioness and rushed after him.

Juliana tried to prepare herself for another onslaught, but the marchioness patted her hand. "It's nothing to concern yourself about, my dear. Doubtless his bay gelding will get his share of exercise before the day is over. We at least will have an hour or so of peace and quiet."

"But I feel so badly for having been the source of such trouble. We already have enough on our minds with preparations for the ball."

"We will manage, as always."

"If you like, I will try to make peace with Miles, Lady Grantsby."

"You mean you will promise not to see Sir Alexi again?"

"No." Juliana shook her head slowly. "I'm sorry. I can't give Miles that satisfaction. It wasn't Sir Alexi's fault that we were delayed." She laughed without humor. "The truth of it is that I had already decided not to see him again. To do so would only serve to encourage him, and I have no interest whatsoever in continuing the relationship."

The marchioness smiled. "Juliana, you are a stubborn woman."

"I fear you are right."

"Very much like myself, I think."

Juliana looked up in surprise. "You are far too kind to me in your comparison."

"Not at all."

For the first time since Juliana met her, the marchioness allowed herself the luxury of leaning back against the chair in a relaxed position. "No, Juliana. I do not expect you to placate Miles if it goes against your judgment. But you are a woman, and not completely without experience when it comes to men. Miles is acting like a jealous suitor. You can find a way to soothe him."

Lady Grantsby fluttered her fan in front of her face, then looked slyly over the lace-trimmed edge. "At night when you are seated on the floor beside the peephole would be a splendid opportunity, wouldn't you say?"

Juliana was aghast. "You...you know about that?"

"Of course, child. I've known about the peephole since Miles and Archibald were young boys. The fireplace draft leads directly into my chambers on the floor below, and the sound carries quite nicely." She folded her fan and let it hang from her wrist by a silken cord. "Miles is by far too full of life to let pass such an opportunity to speak to you without the intrusion of a chaperon."

Juliana swallowed. "You heard every word, your ladyship?"

"Every word."

Juliana tried swiftly to recall what she might have said that could prove embarrassing, but the marchioness read her mind.

"You have nothing to fear, Juliana. I've come to know that I can trust you. That is not to say that I completely approve of your relentless desire for independence." She took a slow sip of sherry from the fragile crystal glass, then leaned forward.

"I hope my confidence has not added to your embarrassment, Juliana. I have no intention of speaking of this to Miles, nor will I mention it again to you."

They were interrupted shortly thereafter by the butler who wanted to discuss certain household affairs with the marchioness. Juliana took the opportunity to go upstairs to her rooms to change. When she went downstairs again, the house seemed oddly silent. Neither Miles nor Louisa took their place at dinner. The marchioness made no mention of their absence, but Juliana noted that places were set for them at the table. Although she hated to admit it to herself, Juliana could only assume that they were together.

ON THE AFTERNOON before the day of the Princess Ball the houseguests began to arrive in all manner of carriages adorned with family crests, gold filigree, and brilliant lacquer. They were loaded to the limit with portmanteaux, baskets and boxes for the nobs, as well as their considerable entourage. The blooded horses alone were worth a king's ransom.

The ladies were resplendent in furs and velvets elegant enough to have stepped directly off the pages of *La Belle Assemblée*. The men, not to be outdone, were perfumed, curled and polished, according to the latest dictates of the current gentlemen's periodical.

Miles and his mother, along with Louisa, stood ready to greet the first arrivals as they were announced. Juliana had planned to watch the procession of carriages from the oriel window of her sitting room, but the marchioness insisted she stand in the receiving line. Louisa was miffed.

"Isn't it rather inappropriate for a mere houseguest and secretary to wait upon the new arrivals?" Louisa asked. "It seems to me that such a responsibility gives Lady Juliana a recognition that simply doesn't exist."

To Juliana's surprise, it was Miles who set Louisa down. "Lady Louisa," he admonished, "I hardly think standing in the receiving line will give Lady Juliana rights to succession. Indeed, to exclude her would show a marked lack of respect for her position. I'm sure you had not intended such a slight."

Louisa's face turned scarlet. "Certainly not. It is only my wish that the proper protocol be observed."

Juliana would by far have preferred to be an observer rather than a participant. Even so, as each carriage arrived, she strained to see what crest was emblazoned on the side. First there was the Viscount of Glenbrook, his wife the viscountess, and their daughter, Miss Jane Plinkton. It struck Juliana that the very ordinary-looking Miss Plinkton, with her sallow skin and cow eyes, looked strangely out of place when compared to her handsome parents. The viscountess was blessed with glossy black hair, flawless skin, and a profile that could have graced a cameo.

Arriving second were the Baron Montland and his wife, the Right Honourable Lady Montland, and their entourage of nearly a dozen servants. Lady Montland was attractive in her own quiet way, but her husband was the very picture of the distinguished nobleman. His black hair was shot with broad streaks of silver, and his bearing was regal enough to suit even the strictest taskmaster.

They were followed by the Duke and Duchess of Heatherford and their two beautiful children. Despite their lofty positions, the duke and duchess were genuinely cordial to everyone no matter what their situation might be. The duchess' crown of shining auburn hair was the first thing people noticed, but the second thing to impress everyone was the very obvious affection between the four members of the ducal family.

Juliana envied them. She was beginning to enjoy the excitement and polite interchange of pleasantries despite the ever-present threat of the Earl of Fordyce, whom, she concluded, would contrive to make a grand entrance.

The tone was set for the day by the friendliness of the Duke and Duchess of Heatherford, who went to the extreme to make everyone feel at ease in their august presence. The marchioness, looking even more regal than usual in her dove-gray velvet with black beaver rimming the bodice and extending down the front, pulled Juliana aside.

"It's going well, don't you think?"

"Perfectly," Juliana agreed.

"Then be good enough to stop looking over your shoulder."

Juliana tried, but it was difficult to forget the Earl of Fordyce. As the hours passed, she was slowly beginning to hope that a divine providence had kept the earl from keeping his appointment.

Dinner that night was laid out in the gold-paneled refectory. The walls hung with silk pennants representing the house of each family who was to attend the Princess Ball. Juliana's plate was filled from the heavily laden buffet table by Sir Hilary Gordon, a Knight of the Garter and a distant relative of the Count of Bradenburg. He was perhaps in his early forties and a decent-looking man with a massive head of unruly dark hair. He brushed a lock of it away from his eye for the tenth time as he motioned Juliana toward a pair of empty chairs near the wall.

"I would be pleased to return for a glass of wine if you would care for some," he said as he seated her.

"No, thank you, Sir Hilary. Perhaps later." She sat down, and he adjusted his tails and took the chair next to hers.

"Lady Juliana, I deem it an honor to be your escort tonight. I've heard so much about you."

"Indeed?" She turned her gaze full upon him, knowing without asking that her reputation could well have been common gossip as far away as Germany.

"And just what have you heard?" she asked, a defensive edge sharpening her voice.

"That you are an extraordinary woman whose husband was so shortsighted as to prefer the gaming tables when his real prize waited for him at home."

Juliana was taken aback. "You flatter me, sir. I don't know what to say."

"Say nothing, if you like. Your beauty speaks for you."

Juliana laughed. "Come now, Sir Hilary. I know too much when I hear it. What is it you want from me?"

He pretended to look hurt. "What do I want? Only the pleasure of your company, my lady, for surely I cannot hope to compete with other men who have more to offer you than I." He smiled, charming her in spite of herself. "However, should you be looking for a protector or husband, I might be willing to join the competition."

Juliana adjusted the fold of her skirt. "There is no competition, Sir Hilary. I am not looking for a protector, let alone a husband."

He was about to answer when they suddenly became aware that Miles had been listening to them, his face as dark as a moonless night on the Scottish moors. It was obvious he had overheard the last of the conversation.

"Lady Juliana," he said, his voice tightly controlled. "Would you be good enough to come with me to greet our remaining guests."

She rose, putting her plate on a small serving table, then curtsied to Sir Hilary. "Excuse me, please. And thank you for an interesting conversation."

He rose quickly and bowed. "My pleasure, madam. I sincerely hope it will not be our last. Please remember me when you fill out your dance card tomorrow night at the ball."

Miles took Juliana by the elbow and propelled her toward the salon. "Must you make a conquest of every man you meet?"

"Miles, don't be ridiculous. You of all people should realize it is only a game they play."

"Then let the others play the game."

She laughed without real humor. "I find that pathetic, coming from you, Miles. Sometimes I think it is you who invented the game."

"Don't argue, Juliana. Just do as I say."

The intensity of his voice made her look up quickly. She saw the pain written in his eyes and knew, beyond doubt, that this anger was born out of jealousy. She was tempted to tease him, but the thought that he really cared about her was so tantalizing that it stirred something inside her. Her voice softened, and she placed her hand on his arm.

"Forgive me, Miles. It is only that my reputation has preceded me. There isn't a man in the ton who wouldn't faint dead away if I took his offer seriously. It is only because of the gossip that they consider me fair game."

He looked contrite as he briefly covered her hand with his. "You would be well advised to think twice before you take a chance on it. Public opinion is not what it first was when you arrived in London. Haven't you noticed that most of the women here tonight have been watching you with envy rather than disdain?''

"I've taken scant notice." Juliana lifted the edge of her skirt as they negotiated a narrow turn beside a tall pedestal topped with a luxuriant fern fresh from the conservatory. The Duchess of Melbourne inclined her head and smiled warmly as they passed.

"You see," Miles said. "You may still be the topic of conversation, but the tone has changed."

Juliana lifted her shoulder in dismissal. "It matters little, for once I take on a position, I will no longer be a part of society. Of importance now is getting through these festivities so that I may take up my own life for a change."

He tensed. "Do you find it so unpleasant living here?"

"Not entirely. I have grown very fond of your mother."

His eyes narrowed, and he seemed to hold his breath. She could barely hear him when he spoke. "Indeed. Am I to assume that you have little affection for me? I thought for a time, back at the country house, that you might one day come to care for me rather deeply."

His words first warmed, then chilled Juliana. No matter what she felt for him, there was no future here. She must learn to accept that his future was already decided.

"You must not confuse what I felt for you then with the way things are now. At the country house I had no idea you were a gentleman of the ton. You needed me then." She looked him straight in the eyes and lied. "You were twice as enticing as a navvy just in from the sea, than as the lord of the manor. You have far too many interests."

"Is that why you moved the chair in front of the peephole?"

Before she could answer, the marchioness, with Louisa firmly in tow, approached them. "Oh, there you are, my dears. We've been waiting for you to greet our new arrivals. Come, we mustn't keep them waiting."

Juliana, with Miles close behind, followed the marchioness into the petit salon where a group of nobles were sipping sherry. The footman announced first the marchioness, then Miles, Juliana and Louisa in order. Juliana dropped a curtsy, inclining her head slightly as she did so. When she raised her eyes, there, standing directly in front of her, was the Earl of Fordyce.

CHAPTER TWELVE

WHEN THE FULL IMPACT of his presence struck her, Juliana felt as Cedric must have felt the night he was set upon in the mews by ruffians. The Earl of Fordyce made a proper leg and took great care to present a charming facade, but a closer look revealed the cruel streak that lay just below the surface. His curly red hair and sharply pointed beard set him apart from other men, as did his cold gray eyes, which failed to mirror the smile he now bestowed upon her.

"Lady Juliana. What a pleasure it is to meet you."

"Why would you say that, sir?" Her words and tone of voice silenced all conversation, but the earl wasn't intimidated. He smiled, his tiny white teeth showing repulsively.

"What man alive would not consider it a pleasure to meet one so lovely? Indeed, you have become almost as famous as the Princess Charlotte herself."

Juliana's voice was dry. "If that is true, sir, it is the murder of my husband and the theft of my property by your hired thugs that has made my name common gossip. Were it not for you, I would still be at home in Dorset."

His face had begun to darken, but he smiled. "An utter fabrication, of course, but if it were true, then all of London society must be in my debt for having brought you to us."

The man was clever. Juliana tried her best to put him down, but he succeeded in turning each thrust of the knife into his own advantage. Miles put an end to the conversation by drawing the earl into another circle.

The marchioness took Juliana by the elbow and steered her toward the door. "Enough of that, me gal. I promised to keep the two of you apart, but I had no idea you would attack him in the receiving line." She fluttered her fan in front of her face, then snapped it shut and let it fall to her waist. "I'd advise you to stay clear of him, Juliana. He isn't without power, you know. A woman, even a highborn woman such as you, cannot be safe against a scum such as he."

Juliana was visibly shaken. "Thank you for intervening. A moment longer, and I would have clawed the smile off his oily face. I don't understand how Miles can dolly up to the man like that."

The marchioness lifted a shoulder. "Lay it to politics, my dear. Miles usually has a reason behind his actions."

She and the marchioness were immediately surrounded by a group from the northern countries who had been privy to the unfortunate scene. Juliana was aware of a subtle ring of protection surrounding her as they hastened to redirect the conversation.

"What is the latest gossip about Princess Charlotte and the German princeling?" a certain Lady Anne asked, her tiny eyes glittering with undisguised curiosity. "Is it true that the man is penniless and that he's presently renting quarters over a mercantile shop on Bond Street?''

The marchioness nodded. "I'm not certain of the address, but yes, it is more than a rumor." She touched the woman's wrist in a gesture of confidence, which Juliana recognized as a way of instilling trust and putting an end to the rumors concerning the royal family.

"We all are so happy to know, however, that in spite of his temporary lack of funds, Princess Charlotte's financé is quite intelligent, very charming and extremely good-looking. Prinny feels that the prospects are good for an excellent connection.''

Juliana was able to fade into the background as the discussion continued. It was a deliberate move on the part of the marchioness, and Juliana appreciated it, even though she was curious about Lady Grantsby's motives.

A short time later Miles joined the group and succeeded in drawing Juliana slightly apart from the others. His mouth was set in a thin line.

"Woman, are you determined to ruin everything? I have only just now managed to placate the earl with a bottle of my best vintage wine. How much do you expect him to take before he departs bag and baggage?''

Juliana stiffened. "Small loss to most of us, but I had no idea that you were such a champion of the Earl of Fordyce. If you are a friend of his, then you are no friend of mine, Miles Harcourt.''

His eyes smoldered. "You will regret having said that, Juliana. Don't you know by now that what I do, I do only for your own good?"

"That's what my father told me when he sanctioned my betrothal to Cedric."

Miles swore softly and ran a white handkerchief across his brow. "Egad. There are times when you try my patience to the very limit."

She caught her breath at the intensity of his gaze. Her voice shook when she spoke. "Indeed. It has always been so between us. I trust that the time is drawing short when you will no longer have to contend with me. Until then, sir, perhaps it would be wise for us to avoid speaking to each other."

He looked shocked. "God's blood!" He took her hands. "You can't mean that, Juliana."

She wanted to deny it, and tell him that she wanted to spend the rest of her life with him, but she knew she must end it now. Over his shoulder, Juliana saw Louisa watching them with glittering eyes.

Juliana drew her hands quickly away and folded them behind her, as if to keep them safe from his grasp. "At least pay me the respect due me, Miles. Granted, my behavior has from time to time belied my gentle upbringing, but I will not continue to allow you to take advantage of me."

His eyebrows shot upward. "I, take advantage of you?" He swore competently. "If I had taken advantage of you, madam, you would be the first to know."

She shrugged impatiently. "I didn't mean it in that way. From the moment I met you, you have gone out of your way to keep me off-balance. Were it not for you, I would have sailed aboard the *Empress Elaine* and be presently living in the Indies.''

''Yes. As a maid to Lady Penelope,'' he said dryly.

''And what am I now? Better to be a lady's maid than an unwanted houseguest.''

''Is that how you feel?''

''I . . . no. In truth, I no longer feel unwelcome here at Grantsby Hall,'' she said, lowering her gaze.

He lifted her chin with his forefinger. ''There. That's better. I must talk to you alone, Juliana. This isn't a good time, but tonight . . .''

He was about to finish the sentence when Louisa came toward them, her face gone white around the mouth. Juliana looked at Miles. ''Yes. Tonight you and Louisa will no doubt be alone together in your room as you were before.''

He looked appalled. ''You can't be serious. Surely you don't believe that Louisa and I are having an affair.''

Juliana was saved from having to answer when Louisa cut into their conversation.

''What a charming tête-à-tête. Lady Juliana, you do have a penchant for creating situations whenever the house is filled with guests.'' Louisa spoke softly, but there was no denying the venom in her eyes. She wasn't above causing trouble of the worst kind.

Juliana drew herself up sharply. ''If you will excuse me, I have things to do.''

Miles touched her arm. ''Juliana. Trust me, I beg of you. There is nothing . . .'' But Juliana didn't stay long enough to hear what he said. She mingled among the guests long enough to see Miles, his arm across the shoulders of the Earl of Fordyce, disappear into the library with four other men. It was nearly an hour later when it became obvious that they were well into their cups.

Juliana would have given anything to escape to her room, but she knew the marchioness relied upon her to keep the guests circulating. It should have been Louisa's task, but she had retired to her rooms earlier with a throbbing headache.

Except for the six men in the library, the guests had assembled in the drawing room for a musicale, which was followed by arrack punch and cakes. Juliana was standing next to the Duchess of Heatherwood when her senses were overwhelmed by a strong odor of musty wine. She turned, seeing the wide-eyed expression on the duchess' face, and nearly bumped into the Earl of Fordyce.

Juliana attempted to move away, but he put a hand on her shoulder and gripped it painfully. "I'm told you are looking for a position as a maid, pretty lady."

A gasp went around the room. Pain lanced through Juliana's shoulder, and her voice was low and deadly. "Take your hand off me, sir."

He smiled, still charming despite his drunken state. "My apologies, Lady Juliana. It grieves me to kn- know that you are left p-penniless." He moved closer to her until she could feel his fetid breath on her skin as he spoke. "A woman like you need n-never go beg- ging, Juliana. I would take good care of you and pay you very well."

Out of respect to the marchioness, Juliana didn't want to make another scene, but neither the marchioness nor Miles were in evidence. Nor could she ask anyone else to risk danger by coming to her aid.

Once again the earl grasped her shoulder, and she feared that he might tear her gown. Taking little care to make it look like an accident, Juliana dumped the entire contents of her wineglass down the front of his breeches, leaving a wide red stain on the pale blue satin. He jumped back as if shot and let out a howl that brought both Miles and the marchioness in haste.

They both looked oddly alert. Juliana, in heightened awareness to everything that was happening around her, noticed that the marchioness had forgotten her cane. Nevertheless, she moved swiftly and took Juliana's arm.

"My dear, I see you spilled your punch. What an unfortunate accident. Miles, will you see to the earl? Perhaps you might escort him to the library."

The earl, suddenly sober, was obviously furious. "I'll break you for this, countess. Just like I broke your husband. But you won't have it as easy as he, my lady. I'll see you working the streets where sluts like you belong."

The rage that shook his voice reached Juliana to the center of her being, and for the first time she was acutely afraid of him. Miles, on the other hand, was smiling as he led the earl toward the library. They had their arms around each other in a fine show of camaraderie. The assembled guests murmured their displeasure at the behavior of the two men.

The swine, Juliana thought. *Men. They stand together against women.* She caught a quick glimpse of her face in the mirrored wall, and had it not been for the peach gown that she wore, she would not have recognized that white-faced angry woman.

The marchioness showed Juliana to a secluded alcove while she instructed the musicians to begin to play. The guests found chairs, and Juliana was left alone with the marchioness. Once the first rush of fear dissipated, Juliana was left with an overwhelming sadness that Miles could so easily have turned against her.

"How could he do this to me, Lady Grantsby? How could Miles—?"

"Hush," Lady Grantsby insisted. "Miles has his reasons. Go up to your room now and freshen your face."

"Would you excuse me for the rest of the evening?"

"No. I cannot do that. You must come down as soon as you've set yourself to rights. It's important to me, Juliana."

It took some doing, but Juliana knew it was better to face the crowd than to scuttle away to the dark like a wounded animal. Nadina had worked her magic, and when Juliana returned to the drawing room, she looked refreshed, though a trifle pale.

Louisa, apparently recovered from her headache, saw her first and swept over to her in a cloud of white lace and heady perfume. "There you are at last. The marchioness asked me to wait for you. You are wanted in the library."

Juliana sighed. "What is it now?"

"I have no notion, but Miles is there as well as several others." She spoke coldly. "You'd best hurry. It seemed important."

"Are you to be there?"

"No." Louisa's voice was flat, and she turned abruptly and flounced away.

Juliana hesitated for the briefest moment, then headed toward the library. She was too numb to feel anything more than apprehension.

They were gathered around a long table; four men dressed in black, whom she vaguely remembered having met, and Miles, looking arrogant and virile in his ivory waistcoat and breeches. His hands were pressed flat on the table as he bent over the Earl of Fordyce, who was seated at the end. The marchioness, her cane restored to her, sat at the other end of the table, regal and untouched by what had happened, except for a bright-eyed alertness.

She thumped the cane resoundingly. "There you are, Lady Juliana. We've been waiting for you. May I present Mr. Harvey Cromwort, of the office of the local magistrate. I believe you know these other gentlemen, and of course, the Earl of Fordyce."

Except for the earl, they rose and bowed.

Miles spoke for the first time. "I believe Mr. Cromwort has something to tell you. Would you care to sit down, Lady Juliana?"

She shook her head but nevertheless grasped the back of a tall chair for support.

The magistrate, pinching a quizzing-glass in his right eye, remained standing. "Madam. We have, for some time, been investigating the transfer of certain properties belonging to the estate of your husband, the late Sir Cedric Penridge, to the Earl of Fordyce. It seems there was some question about the rightful ownership, as well the unsolved mystery of your husband's untimely death.''

He ahemmed and cleared his throat in a noisy fashion that, in her faint condition, nearly caused Juliana to gag. Then he continued.

"After considerable investigation, a certain Miss Polly Pendergast, a serving wench at the establishment where the wager took place, has been found. She admitted, under penalty of perjury, that your husband had indeed won the wager. She was also good enough to provide us with another witness who has testified to the knowledge that the Earl of Fordyce hired the thugs who waylaid your husband in the mews and ended his life.''

Juliana felt the floor begin to spin around her. Then someone helped her into a chair. The marchioness leaned forward.

"Are you all right, Juliana?''

She nodded. "I don't understand. What does all this mean?''

Miles made a harsh sound. "Mean? Why, it means that the earl has signed a complete confession, and it has been witnessed by the magistrate as well as these lords.''

The magistrate nodded. "It means that the deed to your husband's estate will be restored to you, as well as the casket of gold coins and jewels he won in the toss of the coin.'' He consulted some papers. "And, of course, the deed to a certain importer's shop in Sussex, called the Crown of India."

Juliana looked at Miles. "Is this true?"

He nodded. "Every word. You are a rich woman, Juliana."

Juliana's gaze traveled to the earl, whose eyes burned mercilessly into hers. "And what of him?" she asked.

His grace, the Duke of Heatherwood, grasped the front edges of his waistcoat. "Justice will prevail, your ladyship. He will stand trial and ultimately face the gallows. You need fear him no longer."

Juliana drew a sharp breath and slowly exhaled. "What can I say? Thank you, thank you each one for what you have done for me. I will ever be grateful to you."

It was a short time later that the magistrate's men came to take the earl away. Miles's solicitor was on hand to advise Juliana about legal matters. The deed to her husband's home would be turned over to her at once, and she was free to draw funds from the bank, pending settlement of her affairs.

They had intended to keep the matter quiet, but word soon leaked out, and the guests gathered around Juliana to congratulate her on having bested the earl.

Louisa, though she made a game try, failed to show any enthusiasm. Then, just before Juliana was ready to retire for the night, Louisa pulled her into a corner.

"Forgive me if I have belittled your wonderful good news, Lady Juliana. Suffice it to say that I am so delighted with my own news that I am close to willy-nilly." She smiled slyly. "The truth is . . . Miles and I have decided to announce our betrothal."

Louisa apparently saw the shock written in Juliana's eyes because she clapped her hands. "Yes, yes. Isn't it too much? Of course we shall wait to make it public until after the Princess Ball tomorrow night, but then it will just be a question of days until everyone knows."

Juliana somehow managed to pay the expected congratulations. At her first opportunity she fled to her room and locked the door. It wasn't long after that when she heard the soft scratching that meant Miles was trying to open the peephole. She covered her ears and refused to acknowledge it.

THE EVENING OF THE PRINCESS BALL had arrived, and the staff was surprisingly well prepared. When Juliana rang for Nadina to help her dress, there was a peculiar sparkle of excitement in the abigail's eyes.

"*Pour l'amour de Dieu!* Why such a long face, madam, when you are once again a rich woman?"

Juliana shook her head. "I don't want to talk about it. Fetch the green velvet from the armoire, please. I must get ready." Nadina didn't answer, and Juliana noticed with surprise that the girl had gone into her own room.

Juliana was about to call her when Nadina returned, carrying an exquisite moss-green gown of embroidered Indian silk.

"Madam? What do you think? Do you like it?"

Juliana gasped. "Like it? Why, it's the most incredibly lovely gown I've ever seen. Where did you get it? To whom does it belong?"

"It is yours, Lady Juliana, if you want it. It is simply an old gown of yours that I took the liberty of remaking. The embroidery I did at night after I finished my other duties."

Juliana held it up to herself and turned to look in the empire mirror that stood at the end of the room. Tears filled her eyes. "It is exquisite. But why would you do this for me?"

"It was the only way I have of repaying you for all you have done for me. You will wear it, then?"

Juliana hugged her. "I shouldn't. For even Princess Charlotte will look shoddy next to me." She grinned. "But I will. I can't wait to make my grand entrance."

Later, as she stood before the mirror admiring the full effect, Juliana traced the fine stitchery; a cluster of ivory and cobalt-blue flowers caught up in a pale green frond that swept gracefully from one shoulder across the slim bodice to the opposite hip. The fabric was delicate and fragile, so much so that when she walked it appeared as if she were floating.

Nadina had caught Juliana's hair in a high crown of blond curls that were sprinkled with shining bits of gold dust. Two long curls were allowed to fall free over one bare shoulder.

As Nadina predicted, Juliana was the sensation of the night. Princess Charlotte looked surprisingly attractive, considering her lack of grace and the overuse of heavy purple velvet trimmed with ermine.

Juliana was pleased to note that the girl looked happy with her young German princeling. The evening went well, and both Lady Grantsby and Louisa were in their glory. As for Miles, he seemed a trifle subdued but certainly did not at any one moment lack for female attention. Juliana made a concerted effort to avoid being anywhere near him.

The last twenty or so guests lingered on after the royal family left. The marchioness took the opportunity to sit down. She drew Juliana down beside her.

"And what now, me gal? What will you do now that you are a woman of considerable means? Will you stay in London or return to your former home?"

Juliana pressed her fingertips together in the form of a steeple. "I have made no plans as yet, but one thing I know for sure. I will sell the home that belonged to Cedric. It is quite large and should bring a healthy price. Perhaps I can find another house like your country place. Not so large, of course. But I grew very fond of it because it was a place of happiness for me."

The marchioness thrust out her lower lip. "Why not make an offer on it? The place is going to ruin with no one there to attend to it."

"But surely the house must have been in your family for generations."

"For two, actually. But King's Grant has served its purpose, and we rarely travel to Fordingbridge these days. We have more extensive holdings in Brighton." She fluttered her hands. "So you see, if you are interested, I'm sure the terms would be most satisfactory to you."

Juliana's heart skipped. "I don't know. This is all so new to me. The country house holds so many memories that it frightens me."

"Yes. I can imagine. Memories of a time you might prefer to forget."

"Never! No matter how painful it is to remember, I will never willingly forget the days that Miles and I spent together." Juliana clasped her hands tightly in front of her. "Do you mean it? Would you sell the house? Would Miles even consider the idea?"

"I think Miles would be overjoyed to have you live there. He hates seeing houses go to waste."

"I wonder how soon we could resolve the sale? I would be willing to pay whatever is a fair price."

The marchioness took Juliana's hands in hers. "Child, are you so eager to leave us?"

Juliana nodded, tears glistening in her eyes. "I must. I simply cannot remain here with things the way they are."

"I can see that. I wish that life could be different, but we are so often guided by our destinies. That is the price we pay for being of the nobility. Miles is well aware that the family and its business must come first before our emotional needs." She sighed. "Would your abigail go with you?"

"For the present. Nadina and her young lieutenant plan to marry in a year or so."

"It's not that I want you to go, Juliana, but I can see the urgency in your eyes. If you like, you could leave tomorrow and stay in the country house until you buy it or find a place you prefer."

"Do you think I could?"

The marchioness nodded. "From what our solicitors say, your income from the importer's shop will be substantial. The man who runs it has been doing so for years." She smiled. "You will never have to look for work again. In truth, Juliana, I think it would be a wise move."

"Yes. I can spend my time refurbishing the house, clearing out those lovely old gardens. We could even have a sailboat on the lake...and swans!" She caught herself up short when she saw the marchioness smile.

"Forgive me, my lady. I didn't mean to run on. With your permission I will depart early tomorrow. The solicitor has advanced me sufficient funds so that I can well afford to hire servants." She smiled. "And I am half owner of the coach Miles bought to bring us here. Fortunately, Mr. Carruthers has stayed on. He may be willing to accompany Nadina and me."

"Once you arrive, you can find help in the village to assist you with the work." She smiled. "I'll miss you, Juliana."

"And I, you, but I think it is best that I leave as soon as possible."

"I'll advise the stablemaster of your plans, so he will have the carriage and horses ready."

They continued to talk for a while and then went to say goodbye to the departing guests. Juliana was aware that Miles was holding himself aloof from her, and she couldn't blame him after the way she had dressed him down. She couldn't, in good conscience, leave without saying goodbye to him, but the opportunity failed to present itself.

Later that night in her room, she moved the chaise from in front of the fireplace and lifted the cluster of grapes that covered the peephole.

"Miles, are you there?" Silence. She called again. This time there was movement, and she heard him walk toward the fireplace.

"What is it?" His voice was curt.

"I wanted to say goodbye. I'm leaving tomorrow to go to the country house."

"So I've been told."

There was a heavy silence, and Juliana's heart felt like a cold potato stuck in her throat.

"I . . . hope you don't object to my being there."

"How could I? The house is perfect for you. I know how you feel about it."

"Thank you." Again the silence was so intense that it was almost painful. Then he spoke, and she could hear the emotion in his voice when he said her name.

"Juliana, I . . ."

She failed to hear the rest of it because the telltale rattle of the doorknob warned her that someone had entered her private sitting room.

CHAPTER THIRTEEN

JULIANA'S HEART CAUGHT in her throat until she recognized Martha, Louisa's abigail, standing in the bedroom doorway.

"Beggin' your pardon, mum," she stammered. Her eyes were wide with fear. "I was afraid to knock. Your room being so close to 'is lordship's, and all."

Juliana glanced swiftly behind her to make sure the cluster of grapes covered the peephole. "What is it, Martha? Something is wrong. It is Lady Louisa?"

The woman wrang her hands. "Indade it tis. She left without me tonight. That's what she did. That was hours ago, and she still haint come back."

"Left? I don't understand. Where did she go?"

"It's him she's gone to see, like always. That Spanish count, Don Castillo."

Juliana motioned to the woman to sit down. So that was the answer to Louisa's disappearances. Was he also the man who had torn Louisa's gown the night of the reception? A cold chill ran down Juliana's spine.

"Tell me," she probed. "Did Lady Louisa go alone?"

"Aye. He brought 'is vis-à-vis around in back for her after everyone was gone. I saw him there in his black cape and top hat. It was him, all right."

"Do you know where they went?"

The older woman shrugged. "Where they always go. To 'is cottage over on Marylebone. It's up to no good 'e is, and I'm afeared for 'er ladyship."

"Did he force her to go with him?"

Martha laughed dryly. "Not likely. 'Twould be more like her ladyship to force 'im. She has a fever, that one. He's in 'er blood, and she can't stay away from 'im."

"Surely not," Juliana protested. "Lady Louisa is in love with Miles."

Martha settled her short neck lower into the gray wool shawl that covered her shoulders. "She plans to marry 'is lordship, mum, but she's in love with the Spaniard."

"How long has this been going on?"

"Near on a year now. She pretends to be goin' to guild meetings and such, while all the time she's been meeting 'im. It weren't so bad when she took me wi' her, but tonight she was into 'er cups and wouldna' let me go." Martha grasped Juliana's sleeve in a gesture of entreaty. "Please, Lady Juliana. You must help. You're the only one I can trust. 'Er ladyship told me how you helped her the night she tore 'er dress in the garden."

"You mean when Don Castillo tore her dress?"

"No, mum. He was there, all right, but she tore 'er own dress 'oping to trap 'im into offering for her. But 'e got scairt and run off."

"Why was he frightened?"

"'Tis his family, mum. He says they would never approve of 'im marrying an Englishwoman."

"Oh, bother." Juliana quickly considered the consequences, then made up her mind. "Do you know the place where they've gone? Can you take me there?"

The woman's tiny eyes widened. "You, mum? I thought maybe you could ask 'is lordship to go after her."

"If I do that, Martha, there is bound to be a dreadful confrontation. I think it's better that we go alone.

"Do you know Mr. Carruthers, the coachman who brought me here from the country house?" The woman nodded, and Juliana continued. "Go down to the stable and tell him that I want him to ready the carriage. I'll be down there as soon as I dress."

The abigail looked a little uncertain, and Juliana spoke sharply. "Go now, and tell no one else. We have no time to waste."

Juliana had started to change into one of her old black gowns even before the door had closed behind Martha. She was struggling with the fasteners when Nadina flung open the door.

"*Mon Dieu*, you are really going to fetch her. I guessed as much."

"And why are you fully clothed?" Juliana demanded.

"I'm going with you, of course." One look at her set face told Juliana there was no sense arguing. Nadina finished the last button. "Aren't you going to tell him?" She jerked her head toward the base of the fireplace.

"Emphatically no. He would be after them with loaded pistols."

"A sensible precaution, I'd guess."

"As it happens, I don't own one."

"I do." Nadina pulled a small weapon from inside her velvet muff.

Juliana laughed shakily. "Pray keep it hidden. The very sight of it unnerves me."

CARRUTHERS HAD JUST FINISHED putting the team in harness when they slipped out the back door and approached the stables.

Juliana asked, "Can you find the address in the dark?"

"Speakin' for meself, I'm not sure, but this young lackey says he knows where it is."

"Excellent. Thank you, Mr. Carruthers. I know it's late."

He bobbed his head and handed the three women into the carriage.

They rode for what seemed like an interminably long time until they turned into a narrow street, and Martha sat bolt upright.

"This 'ere's the street. I remember it from the times we came here together."

Juliana moistened her lips. "Will...uh...will they be alone? What I mean is, will there be servants?"

"No, mum. I don't think so. They goes home at night."

Nadina studied the house as the carriage drew to a halt in front of an attractive cottage whose front door was protected by a massive iron gate. "*Mon Dieu.* How do you plan to get in?"

"Why, I'll simply ring the bell," Juliana said.

Nadina laughed. "And you expect them to turn out in their nightclothes to let you in?"

Juliana pulled her cloak about her. "I'll face that when I have to."

The driver scuttled around to open the door for them and let down the step while the lackey held the horses' heads. "Mayhap your ladyship would like me to go with her?" Carruthers asked.

Juliana was tempted, but she shook her head. "Thank you, no. Just keep the horses in readiness." Then she turned to the abigails. "Perhaps it would be prudent for the two of you to wait in the carriage."

Nadina said something that shocked Juliana, then apologized. "I refuse to permit you to go in there alone, madam, so shall we proceed?"

"'Tis my lady we aim to protect. I'll not be left behind," Martha stated flatly.

"All right. So be it," Juliana said as she started up the walk. The bellpull was to the right of the iron door, and Juliana gave it a yank. It took four more pulls of the rope before they heard movement inside and saw a man carrying a lamp come toward the door.

"You see," Juliana said. "All you have to do is ring the bell."

"*Mon Dieu!*" Nadina whispered.

The door opened a crack, and a deep masculine voice demanded to know who was there.

"Lady Juliana Penridge. Open the door at once. I've come to fetch Lady Louisa, and I shan't leave until I talk to her."

There was a muffled exchange on the other side of the door, and then it creaked open. The women stepped back as he slid aside the iron gate and motioned them inside.

He was, Juliana noticed with gratitude, only in a mild state of dishabille. He was an extremely handsome young man. Great masses of black hair stuck out at odd angles, and he had shed his coat for a smoking jacket.

"Madam." He bowed. "I trust you have a good reason for this intrusion."

"Indeed. Where is Lady Louisa?"

"She is occupied with friends at the moment and does not wish to be disturbed."

"I cannot accept that. Take me to her at once. You must realize that she is being compromised by this terrible indiscretion."

"My regrets, madam. I cannot go against her wishes."

"If you refuse to take me to her I can only assume that she is being held here against her will." Juliana felt a nudge in her side and looked down to see that Nadina was handing her the pistol. She took it and pointed it at the man's heart.

"As you see, Don Castillo, I am armed. I'd advise you to do as I say."

He looked taken aback, but then a slow smile spread across his face, and for the first time Juliana understood how Louisa could become smitten with the man. His eyes softened as they seemed to caress Juliana's face.

"I admire your courage, ladies, but you should never point an empty pistol." As Juliana looked down in confusion, he gently relieved her of the weapon. Putting it on the table, he took Juliana's hands in his.

"It distresses me, *señora*, that you think so badly of me. I have nothing but the highest regard for Lady Louisa. By all that is holy, she is the light of my heart. I would never harm her. Never!"

Juliana was impressed by his sincerity, but she pulled back. "Harming Louisa is precisely what you have done by bringing her here. And I understand this is not the first time."

He nodded reluctantly, folding his hands in front of him. Juliana could swear she saw the glitter of tears in his eyes, and she felt a twinge of compassion. Then Martha muttered something incomprehensible, and Juliana realized she was losing control of the situation. She made an effort to look stern.

"Don Castillo, I must insist that you take us to Louisa at once."

He sighed. "Perhaps you are right, though. If you will come this way, I will take you to her ladyship."

They followed him to a large bedchamber where Louisa lay sprawled on top of the coverlet, her hair in disarray and her bodice askew. Martha rushed to her and fell at her side.

"Child, what has 'e done to you? I'll tear 'is heart out if 'e has so much as touched you."

Louisa sat up quickly, looked around in confusion, grasped her head in both hands and fell back on the bed with a shuddering groan.

Martha's mouth dropped. "Saints protect us. She's really foxed. I've never seen 'er so bad before."

The heady smell of wine left no doubt that Martha was right. Juliana fixed the Spanish nobleman with an accusing stare. "If you've harmed her or touched her in any way, the marquis will have your head for it."

His eyes betrayed no fear but only deep concern. "I give you my word as a gentleman. The lady is not yet compromised. She was well into her cups before I brought her here. Believe me, Lady Juliana, I love her. We only intended to— And then..." He spread his hands.

Juliana silenced him. "Enough. You must help me get her to the carriage."

That was easier said than done. Louisa, small though she was, lay as limp as a wet thread. It was all they could do to get her into the carriage. Once it was accomplished, Juliana ordered Carruthers to drive at top speed in order to arrive home before the servants wakened for the early morning chores.

Don Castillo held on to the carriage door. "Please, Lady Juliana. Let me come with you."

"Don't be absurd. The marquis would kill you." Then her voice softened. "I'll see that word is sent to you concerning her condition."

He stepped back and bowed. "For that I am indebted to you."

Once the carriage was moving, Louisa lay back against the cushions, her face turned toward the outside wall. She groaned. "I suppose you'll spread this all over London."

Juliana squeezed Martha's shoulder. "Not one of us will breathe a word."

"You must think I'm a fool."

"No. Are you in love with him?"

Louisa's laugh sounded like the crackling of a dry leaf. "What does it matter? Don Castillo would never d-defy his parents. He comes from a very old and es-established Spanish family. They are as rigid as a . . ." Her voice trailed off into nothing, and she slept for a time.

Finally the night air revived Louisa enough that with assistance from the three women she was able to walk upstairs to her bedchamber. Juliana left Louisa in the care of her abigail after cautioning all those involved to keep their silence. By the time Juliana and Nadina returned to their own rooms, the sun was already creeping over the horizon.

Neither Juliana nor Nadina could relax enough to go to bed. Instead, they finished packing for the trip to the country house.

"Are you sure you want to come with me, Nadina?" Juliana probed. "It will be much more difficult for you to see your young lieutenant."

"*Oui*. I know. But we will manage. He is away now and will not return for another fortnight. I will leave a message for him."

Juliana sighed, knowing that if it were she who was betrothed to Miles, there would be no question of her leaving. Was Nadina that sure of herself and her fiancé? She envied them their certainty, their trust.

When she went downstairs for breakfast later that morning, the marchioness was alone at the table, attacking a plate of hot scones and honey.

"Sit down, Juliana. I see you've donned a traveling dress. Does that mean you will soon be ready to leave?"

Juliana waited while the footman poured a cup of steaming chocolate into her cup. "Everything is in readiness. I didn't sleep well last night, so Nadina and I rose early and packed our trunks."

All the time she was speaking, Juliana watched the marchioness to see if she were aware of last night's episode with Louisa. There was not the slightest flicker of eyelid or the least tremor of voice. Was it possible that she didn't know? Juliana fervently hoped so for all their sakes.

"Juliana, my dear, I must confess I'm having second thoughts. I do regret your leaving us. Miles does, too, of course. He was an absolute bear before he left this morning."

Juliana felt dead inside. So he hadn't cared enough to wait and say goodbye. Well, maybe it was better to put an end to that part of her life. No sense in lingering over farewells. She sipped her chocolate and carefully set the cup down.

"And Louisa. Does she know that I'm leaving?"

"Not likely. Martha came downstairs this morning with a message that Louisa was suffering another of her headaches. I expect she will remain in bed most of the day."

Juliana nodded. "I trust you will extend my best wishes to the two of them."

"Of course. Remember, Juliana, that you will always be welcome here at Grantsby Hall."

THERE WAS LITTLE to be said after that. Juliana bid her goodbyes to the household staff, and then they were on their way. The carriage had been freshly lacquered and the inside given a good scrub, thanks to Carruthers. Nadina was in high spirits. Her enthusiasm for the trip infected Juliana after a while, and the time flew by quickly. They spent the night at the Inn of Two Lions; a decided improvement over the Inn of the Golden Harp where Juliana had met Nadina. They laughed about their first encounter, and Nadina's effect on Miles. But mentioning Miles's name made Juliana melancholy.

It was late the following afternoon when they arrived at the country house. Nadina nearly fell when Carruthers helped her down from the carriage.

"*Mon Dieu.* I had no idea the house was so large."

Juliana looked around her. "And I had forgotten that it was so neglected. The grounds look like a jungle even for this time of year. Heaven knows what it will be like in the summer."

Carruthers stroked his chin. "Aye. A handy crew o' workers will clean it up in no time. I've some nephews who can wield a good hoe."

He had already been given instructions to ask in the village about a temporary housekeeper, but for the time being the two women were content to do for themselves.

Juliana smiled, and Nadina put her hands on her hips.

"Now that is much better, madam. It is good to see you smile."

Juliana laughed. "It's the house. It has that effect on me." She thrust the iron key into the massive lock. "The last time I arrived here, I broke a window to get in."

Nadina's eyes widened. "*Non.* I can't believe it. Someday, madam, you must tell me all about it."

Juliana shook her head. "No. I don't think so."

Nadina saw the tears glistening in Juliana's eyes, and she didn't press the issue. Instead she bustled around, hanging up coats, lifting dust covers, and generally taking charge.

Juliana walked around as if in a trance. Everything she touched, every picture, every piece of furniture, brought back memories of Miles and their time together.

In the library where she and Miles had dined so cozily, she opened the draft in the fireplace and lit the tinder. The heat and light from the fire soon dispelled the gloom of closed shutters. *Tomorrow,* Juliana vowed silently, *I'll open those shutters and let in the sunshine.*

She pulled back the draperies and noticed that one shutter hung loose on its hinges. Outside, the limbs from an ancient beech tree grew close to the house. On one of them an abandoned bird's nest clung to the budding branches.

Through the branches Juliana's gaze was caught by something moving in the lane: a dark shape, nearly indistinguishable in the encroaching twilight. She looked carefully. It appeared to be moving closer. A deer perhaps, or a very large dog? Or—her heart nearly stopped—a poacher. Yes, it was the figure of a man in dark clothing.

She wanted to call to Nadina, but the girl was putting clean sheets on the beds in the other end of the house. Had Nadina brought her little pistol along?

Juliana pressed her face close to the window. If only she could see better. There was something oddly familiar about the man. His clothing fit rather snugly on a frame that was muscular and well proportioned.

He walked faster as he neared the house and slung the bag he was carrying from one shoulder to the other. It looked like a seabag.

But what would a sailor be doing . . . ?

"Miles," she said softly. "Miles!" This time she shouted his name as she grabbed the end of her skirt and ran toward the stairs.

Her heels clattered on the wide staircase as she nearly flew down the last flight into the foyer and flung aside the great oaken doors. He saw her then and waved.

Juliana turned suddenly shy as she lifted her hand in response. What did it mean? Why was he here? She willed herself to wait for him, when all the time she wanted only to run into the warmth of his arms.

It seemed to take forever for him to walk the distance from the end of the lane into the semicircular drive. Not once did he look aside or take his gaze away from hers. It was as if an invisible ribbon held them together. Each second the distance between them grew shorter.

And then he was at the bottom of the steps, looking up at her.

"Juliana," he whispered, his voice ragged with deep emotion.

"M-Miles. Wh-what are you doing here?" It was all she could think of to say.

"My God, Juliana. Can't you guess?"

He swung the seabag from his shoulder, and it hit the wooden steps with a dull thud. "I love you, Juliana, and I think you love me. Tell me if I'm wrong, and I won't come a step farther."

Juliana wrapped her arms around herself in an unconscious gesture of self-protection. "Please, Miles, you shouldn't have come."

He came up the steps until he was standing just a few feet away from her. "I asked you a question."

"It's one I'm not prepared to answer."

"The devil take it. Either you love me or you don't." She saw the old familiar fire light his eyes, and her temper flared to match his.

"I'll thank you not to bully me, Miles. I am no longer answerable to you. Does the marchioness know you are here?"

He swore fluently. "What on earth does that have to do with anything?"

"You have a tradition to uphold, Miles."

"If you must know, I have my mother's blessing." He smiled. "And you, of all people, must know how hard that is to come by. She thinks you would make a perfect daughter-in-law, as well as a regal marchioness."

Juliana drew a deep breath and slowly exhaled. "Does that mean you are asking me to marry you?"

"Yes." He held out his arms, and she came into them with a tiny cry of joy.

"Does that mean you will accept?"

"Yes." She pulled back reluctantly and studied his face. "But what about Louisa? The family tradition?"

"Louisa is not in love with me nor I with her. She is infatuated with a certain Don Castillo, a fact of which you are quite aware."

Juliana blushed. "You know about that night?"

"Everyone does. Suffice it to say that I spoke to the Spaniard, and he has agreed to offer for her hand in marriage. It was just the push he needed. They love each other very much, but he hesitated because of his family. Now he is determined to confront them.

"Juliana," he whispered against her hair. "Why are we standing out here?"

She laughed shakily. "There is one very good reason, Miles."

He pulled back and looked at her, a frown crossing his face. "A reason? Dear God, Juliana. Don't tell me there is something else to keep us apart."

She smiled. "Not for long, Miles, but I must warn you, we will not forget convention simply because we are betrothed. We must always be properly chaperoned, so as not to bring scandal down on our family."

He grinned. "No need to worry, my love." He reached into his jacket and pulled out a very bedraggled rag doll. "Remember Mrs. Frobisher, our chaperon?"

Juliana clasped her hands in delight. "Where did you find her?"

"You left her behind. She looked very lonely sitting on the mantel in your old room."

"I didn't expect to need her, And seeing her every day would have made me sad."

"Don't you agree that she will suffice as a chaperon until we can meet with the vicar and declare our vows?"

Juliana sighed. "You are a devious man, Miles Harcourt. Is it this house that brings out that side of your personality? And what are you doing in those ridiculous clothes? I thought for a moment it was a case of déjà vu."

He grinned. "Think back. You told me once that you liked me better when I needed you, as a sailor just in from the sea. I still need you, Juliana, and I didn't want to take any chances. When I asked you to marry me, I wanted to be sure you wouldn't refuse."

"Refuse?" Her eyes filled with tears. "Never, Miles. Never in a million years."

He pulled her against him and kissed her, softly at first but with ever increasing urgency. Juliana met his desire with a passion too long denied. Out of the corner of her eye she saw him reach down and toss the rag doll into the bushes out of sight.

**For the millions who can't read
Give the Gift of Literacy**

One out of five adults in North America
cannot read or write well enough
to fill out a job application
or understand the directions on a bottle of medicine.

**You can change all this by joining the fight
against illiteracy.**

For more information write to:
Contact, Box 81826, Lincoln, Neb. 68501
In the United States, call toll free: 800-228-3225

**The only degree you need
is a degree of caring**

Take 4 best-selling love stories FREE
Plus get a FREE surprise gift!